TALES OF
ROBIN HOOD

TALES OF
ROBIN HOOD

RETOLD BY
TONY ALLAN

ILLUSTRATED BY
RON TINER

EDITED BY FELICITY BROOKS

DESIGNED BY KATHY WARD

SERIES DESIGNER: AMANDA BARLOW

First published in 1995 by Usborne Publishing Ltd,
83-85 Saffron Hill, London EC1N 8RT.
First published in America March 1996.

Printed in Spain.

CONTENTS

how RObert of locksley became an outlaw

It was a fine spring morning in Sherwood Forest, and sunlight filled the clearing where Much the miller lived. Outside the mill stood a row of carts. That was only normal. Much was a popular figure in that part of Nottinghamshire, and he was rarely short of customers.

So there was nothing at all unusual about the sound of horses approaching the clearing ~ or there wouldn't have been if they'd been coming with the slow clip-clop of carthorses pulling wagons laden with corn. But these steeds were galloping, and a jangling of metal on metal indicated that their riders were armed.

The peasants standing by the carts stirred uneasily. Times were hard that spring. It had been four years since King Richard had left England to fight in the Holy Land. For months now there had been no news of him, and stories were spreading that he had been captured and might never come back again.

In Richard's absence, the king's hated brother, John, had become the country's ruler. His tax collectors had been combing the land, leaving ruin and devastation in their wake. It was a time when people had reason to fear the sound of armed men.

Sure enough, half a dozen knights in chain mail soon galloped into the clearing. They spurred up to the mill and reined in their horses in a cloud of dust.

"Whose place is this?" the lead rider shouted. A big, red-faced man came to the door, blinking in the sunlight. If the arrival of the armed men alarmed him, he didn't let it show.

"Mine," he said briefly. Then gesturing towards the soldiers, he added, "But you've got no corn to grind. What's your business with me?"

The rider looked him up and down. He was a thin-lipped man

with a piercing stare, and he wore a scarlet cape over his chain mail.

"Well, miller," he said finally, "it's not grain we want from you. It's information. I hear you've had dealings with a bandit we've been hunting ~ a common thief who calls himself Robin Hood. We mean to hang him. And if you can help us put a rope around his neck, you'll find yourself a richer man."

The miller raised his arm to keep the sun out of his eyes.

"It's true Robin Hood has passed this way," he replied. "But people around here don't call him a bandit. He pays his way like any honest man."

"Watch what you're saying, miller," the horseman warned. "Hood's a known villain. He's stolen the purses off plenty of travelers in Sherwood before. But now he's gone too far. He attacked the tax collectors sent by Prince John."

The miller stood his ground. He was master of his mill, and on his home patch he was used to speaking his mind.

"Tax collectors!" he said. "They're the only thieves we've seen in these parts. They'll go into a man's house and take everything he owns. Tax collectors!" he spat on the ground. "Bloodsuckers, more likely."

The rider's eyes narrowed. "So our tax collectors bleed you dry, do they?" he asked sarcastically. "But by the size of your belly you seem well enough fed."

"I have my mill for a living," Much conceded. "But there are people in the forest who haven't even a crust of bread. The nobles come to the forest to hunt the deer while the poor folk go hungry. It's not easy for men or women to stand by and see their children starve."

There was a murmur of agreement from the people waiting outside the mill. At a sign from the cloaked figure, the horsemen wheeled around upon them.

"Silence!" one cried. "Silence for the Sheriff of Nottingham! The Sheriff rides on Prince John's business. Is there anyone here who dares challenge the Prince's will?"

The crowd fell silent, their heads cast down. Only the miller kept his eyes unflinchingly on the Sheriff. Meanwhile, the sound of voices had drawn someone else from the mill. It was Much's son, Dickon. He gazed in bewilderment at the stilled crowd and the armed men. The Sheriff muttered something and the soldiers turned back toward the burly man. Instinctively, Much put an arm around his son's shoulder,

"WATCH WHAT YOU'RE SAYING, MILLER," THE HORSEMAN WARNED

drawing the boy to him in a protective embrace.

The Sheriff leaned toward Much. "So you don't like the tax collectors and you don't like the nobles," he said. His voice was quieter now, but it cut through the stillness like a knife. "Tell me, miller ~ how do you like Prince John?" The miller shifted uncomfortably.

"I'm a loyal subject of the king," he replied at last.

"And of Prince John, his lawfully appointed deputy?" the Sheriff asked again. The miller remained silent, and as the silence lengthened the soldiers drew their swords.

"I'll give you one more chance, peasant," the Sheriff said, his voice so low now that it was almost a hiss. "Will you, here before these people, swear loyalty to Prince John and all who do his service, be they tax collectors, sheriffs or even fiends from Hell, if he so chose?"

Much pulled himself up to his full height. With his eyes still on the Sheriff's, he proclaimed defiantly, "I swear loyalty to Richard Lionheart, King of England, God bless him. He and no other is my rightful ruler."

"You cur," the Sheriff said contemptuously. Then he turned to the soldiers. "Kill him," he said.

Before Much could even turn to defend himself, the leader of the troop was on him. The sword slid into his chest like a knife into butter. The big man slumped lifeless on the steps of his own mill.

For a moment, Dickon stood stock still, too startled by the horror of what had happened to react. Then with a bound he threw himself on his father's killer, beating helplessly with his bare hands on the soldier's chain mail vest. With one blow of a mailed gauntlet, the rider sent him flying to the ground. The boy lay there, sobbing.

The Sheriff turned to face the crowd. "You've seen what happens to enemies of Prince John," he informed them coolly, without a trace of remorse or even anger in his voice. "And that's what's waiting for the robber Robin Hood. Anyone who helps track him down will be rewarded. You have my word. The Prince knows how to look after his own."

Then, at a sign from the Sheriff, the armed band turned to go. They trotted along the road out of the clearing, leaving the miller's body slumped on the steps and the peasants rooted to the spot, too stunned by what had happened to react in any way.

One man, braver than the rest, finally stepped forward to comfort the weeping Dickon.

"Come with me, lad," he told him gently. "I know a place where they'll look after you ~ and all the more willingly after what's happened here today."

Unseen by his companions, another onlooker had also made a move. While the others gaped, he had slipped out of the clearing at the moment of the killing. He was a thin man with a sallow face and a nervous manner. He took a short cut through the undergrowth to the track by which the Sheriff and his men were leaving, and was waiting for them by the roadside when they rode by.

A soldier asked him roughly what he wanted. The man looked around furtively to make sure no other eyes were on him, then said in a low voice,

"I have some information. Information about Robin Hood."

The Sheriff reined in his mount.

"Let's hear it, then," he said shortly. "Tell us who you are and what you know."

"My name's Wurman, your Honor," the man replied. "I serve Robert of Locksley, the owner of Locksley Hall. And I've heard talk at the Hall ~ things I wasn't meant to hear. I can't tell you who Hood is or where you can find him, but I can say my master knows more about him than any loyal subject of the Prince should know."

"Robert of Locksley," the Sheriff repeated thoughtfully. "I know him, and he's no friend of ours. But he's a well-connected man. I'd need more than servants' gossip to take action against the likes of him."

"Then send someone to the Hall this evening," Wurman responded eagerly. "You'll never have a better chance. My master's to be married tomorrow, to Lord Fitzwalter's daughter Marian, and tonight he's holding open house. Any stranger will be welcome. And when he and his friends are carousing, you never know what secrets might come out."

The Sheriff thought for a moment. "Maybe I'll take your advice," he said, and spurred his horse away down the path.

"And the reward, my Lord?" Wurman called out anxiously after him.

"You'll be taken care of, if what you've told us is true," the Sheriff shouted back, adding as an afterthought, "only remember ~ if you're not more loyal to me than you have been to your master, my dogs will have your bones for breakfast." Then the horses turned out of view.

In fact the Sheriff had already decided to follow Wurman's suggestion, and by the time he got back to Nottingham he had someone in mind for the job. The man that he chose was Guy of Gisborne, the landless second son of a local nobleman. Guy was ambitious, and the Sheriff knew he could be counted on to do his bidding, however cruel, if there was any gain to be had from doing so.

And so it was that Guy, disguised in an ankle-length cloak and carrying a long pilgrim's staff, went to visit Locksley Hall that evening. And a wild evening it was, for Robert was a generous host and half the inhabitants of Nottinghamshire seemed to have come as his guests. There was feasting and toasting and barrels of wine. To entertain the assembled company, minstrels plucked lyres, jugglers juggled and acrobats turned cartwheels and performed balancing tricks.

Presiding over the merriment from the table at the head of the Hall were Robert, an alert, dark-haired man with a half smile always on his lips, and his bride-to-be,

Marian Fitzwalter. Anyone could see that she was beautiful, but after one long, covetous look, Guy of Gisborne decided she was more than that. With her flowing brown hair and flashing eyes, she was quite simply the loveliest woman he had ever seen.

As the evening wore on and the wine and ale flowed, the talk grew freer. Toast after toast was drunk to good King Richard, but Guy heard nothing but curses from his table companions for Prince John. Each guest, it seemed, had his or her own story to tell of the greed of his tax collectors and the cruelty of his forest wardens, who would think nothing of having a man hanged for no more than taking meat to feed his family from the carcass of one of the Prince's deer.

Guy had heard enough by the end of the evening to convince him that Robert was no loyal servant of the Prince, but he still had no evidence that he was in league with Robin Hood. But as he rose to leave, one of the servants caught his eye, jerking his head to indicate that he should follow him out of the Hall. It was Wurman.

Looking around quickly to check that no one was watching, Guy followed him down an empty passageway. The two turned up a spiral staircase that took them to the living quarters of the manor.

Wurman stopped outside a thick oak door. He glanced inside the room briefly, then stepped back. "Take a look," he whispered. Guy pushed open the door. A small figure lay huddled on a pallet of straw laid down on the flagstones in a corner of the chamber. It was Dickon, worn out by weeping for his dead father.

As they made their way back down the stairs, Wurman explained who the boy was and what had happened in the wood that morning. Guy shrugged, unconvinced. "It's odd the boy was brought here, but it's hardly proof of treason," he said. Wurman leaned toward him urgently. "But I was there when he arrived," he whispered, "and I heard what the man who brought him had to say. He said he had a new recruit ~ a recruit for Hood's band."

Back in Nottingham, the Sheriff needed no further proof. In his own mind he'd already decided to move against Robert, and Dickon's presence at the Hall and the remark Wurman claimed to have overheard were evidence enough for him. He and Guy decided then and there on the action to be taken.

The next morning, the church on the Locksley estate was crowded for Robert and Marian's wedding. Knights from the surrounding lands in fur-lined robes escorted ladies dressed in finest muslin. Squires and tenants crowded the aisles and the empty spaces at the back of the church, where Robert's steward, a powerfully-built man named Will Scathlock, stood by the door to welcome guests.

Excited choristers joked with one another while they waited for the ceremony to begin. The part of the church where they were sitting was suffused in a dim, religious glow, cast by recently installed stained glass windows. By contrast, the rest of the building was bathed in bright light, streaming through the old plain glass. To pass the time, guests in the congregation argued the case for and against the new windows.

The vicar entered the church, and the people crowding the aisle squeezed aside to make a path for him. Robert, who had been standing quietly at the back of the church, followed him to the altar-rail to wait for his bride.

He didn't have long to wait. A fanfare sounded, and the Lady Marian entered the church at the side of her father. Once more the aisle was cleared, and the two made their way to where Robert was standing. He took Marian's hand, and her father stepped back to take his place in the front pew.

Robert and Marian looked into one another's eyes, then stepped forward for the ceremony to begin. The vicar turned to meet them. An expectant hush fell over the congregation.

Suddenly the silence was broken by cries from outside the building. The doors of the church were thrown back, and a dozen armed men forced their way in at sword's point. At their head was Guy of Gisborne. Pointing at the bridegroom, he shouted, "Stop the wedding! Robert of Locksley, you're a traitor. I arrest you in the name of Prince John!"

Robert turned to face him across the packed church.
"A traitor to John I may be,"

"STOP THE WEDDING! ROBERT OF LOCKSLEY, YOU'RE A TRAITOR."

he shouted scornfully, "but no man living dares call me a traitor to Richard, our king. What evidence can you bring against me?"

"Evidence enough to hang you, Locksley," the armored man cried. "I accuse you first of being an associate of the bandit and traitor Robin Hood."

"An associate of Robin Hood!" Robert laughed out loud. "Well, I'd be glad enough to be one, if I could. But there's little chance of that, since I *am* Robin!"

There was a moment of silence in the church as the words sank in, followed by a buzz of astonished voices. Friends of Robert moved to block the already crowded aisle against the armed men.

Over the hubbub, Guy of Gisborne's voice could be heard calling on the bridegroom to surrender peacefully.

Robert pressed Marian's hand in a brief gesture of farewell. Leaping onto a pew where the whole congregation could see him, he made a sign to Will Scathlock and cried to Guy, "You'll have to catch me first!" Then, snatching a cloak from a startled guest, he wrapped it loosely around his head and arms and hurled himself head-first through one of the soon-to-be-replaced plain-glass windows.

Pandemonium broke out in the church as the shattered glass rained down behind him. Women were screaming and half the men were waving their arms and shouting. Some of Guy's men tried to force their way to the window, but they could make only slow progress down the packed aisle. Others made for the door to catch the fleeing man. But Will, alerted by his master's gesture, had slipped outside and jammed it shut with the heavy wooden beam that served to secure it.

By the time one of the soldiers had finally managed to clamber out of the broken window and had unjammed the door, Robert of Locksley was riding at full gallop, with Will at his side, along the road to Sherwood Forest. Only now he was no longer Robert of Locksley but Robin Hood, rebel leader, and he was leaving his past behind to begin a new life beyond the frontiers of the law.

the FOREST PEOPLE

News of Robin's flight to the forest quickly spread around the district, and recruits soon started drifting in to join his band. Times were becoming harder throughout the country as Prince John grew ever more greedy and tyrannical, and nowhere were they worse than around Nottingham.

The Sheriff's injustices spread a pall of blood across the countryside. Men had their hands cut off for stealing a loaf of bread; in the royal hunting forests, hungry peasants were hanged for dragging off dead game. For the desperate, only one choice remained: to join the outlaws. The worse things became, the more people found their way to Sherwood.

To start with, the newcomers were often more of a hindrance than a help. Most were peasants better used to driving a plow than living off what the forest provided. Robin had been roaming the woods on his father's estate since he was a child and had learned his woodcraft from the foresters there. Now he had to find ways of passing on the knowledge.

He taught the new arrivals which roots and berries were good to eat and which were poisonous. They learned to recognize the sounds of different birds and animals moving through the forest, so they could tell them instantly from the sound of human foot-steps. They practiced tracking, learning how to move noiselessly through the undergrowth using bushes and tree trunks for cover. After a month's instruction, they knew just about enough to get by, but they were still no one's idea of expert woodsmen.

Robin was wandering through the forest one morning wondering what to do about them when he had an unexpected encounter. Coming out of a thicket onto the bank of a stream, he saw a huge man striding purposefully along the opposite bank just a few paces ahead of him. Robin's policy was never to let strangers pass through Sherwood without finding out who they were and why they were there, so he made up his mind to overtake the traveler and ask him his business.

There was a crossing over the stream not far ahead, so Robin quickened his step, aiming to cut the man off. But he soon realized the stranger had speeded up too, and was matching him stride for stride. The two men reached the opposite ends of the bridge at exactly the same moment. In truth it wasn't so much a bridge as a couple of logs laid across the water, and it was only wide enough to take a single person. So one of them would have to give way.

Seen head on, the stranger was even more formidable than he had looked in profile at first sight. He was half a head taller than Robin, and he had forearms the size of hams. To make things worse, he was carrying a long, iron-tipped staff.

But it took more than size to overawe Robin Hood. In firm tones he said, "Stand back, stranger. I was first onto this bridge."

The other man took no notice of Robin's warning. He just kept on walking until he reached the middle of the logs. Then he stopped and looked down at his opponent.

"I claim right of way," he said flatly, "and for one good reason." So saying, he brandished his staff at the unarmed Robin.

"It's true I have no staff," Robin conceded. "But let me cut one, and we could settle the matter justly."

The big man shrugged his shoulders with the resigned air of someone used to having to put up with other people's foolishness, and Robin went in search of a weapon. He soon found a stout sapling and stripped off its branches. Then he returned to face his opponent.

For a few seconds the two men stood looking at one another, each waiting for the other to make the first move. Then Robin swung his staff full length at the big man's head. If he'd hoped to catch him unaware he was disappointed, because the stranger deflected the blow without even flinching. Then he pushed forward with his own staff, forcing Robin to step back a couple of paces to regain his balance.

Following up his advantage, the stranger swung his staff at Robin, who expertly ducked the blow and retaliated by setting his staff sideways and driving one end with all his might into his rival's stomach. This time he struck home. The big man grunted.

Emboldened by success, Robin stepped forward, aiming for the stomach for a second time. It was a mistake. The stranger pushed the offending weapon away as if it were a twig, throwing Robin off balance as he did so. Then he raised his own staff and caught Robin with a stunning blow behind the ear, sending him tumbling off the bridge into the water.

Robin reappeared spluttering, standing waist-deep in the stream. He looked around wildly for his staff, only to see it floating away out of reach downstream. For an instant he made as if to chase it, but then suddenly, looking down at his dripping clothes, he began to laugh instead. Magnanimously, the stranger reached out a huge hand and helped him back up onto the bridge.

"It looks as though you've made your point," Robin said. He made a mock bow to his rival, and stepped back onto the bank. "I'll gladly grant you right of way," he declared. "Let no one say Robin Hood is a bad loser."

"Robin Hood!" The big man scratched his head, perplexed. "It was Robin Hood I was coming to see." He looked almost sheepish now. "I've been thrown off my lands by the tax collectors, you see," he added. "I thought you might be able to use another helper."

Now it was Robin's turn to be gracious. "How can I say no when you've just pushed me into the river?" he joked. Then in a more serious tone he added, "If you're half as good with a bow and arrow or a sword as you are with a quarterstaff, you might be just the man I'm looking for. But tell me ~ what's your name?"

"Little," the big man said. Robin burst out laughing. "Little?" he repeated incredulously.

"That's right. Little. John Little."

"We mostly take new names in the forest," Robin told him, "but yours is too good to lose. So let's just make it Little John instead." And so John Little got a new name and Robin acquired a valuable new helper.

The newcomer turned out to be exactly what Robin needed to whip his band into shape. He was expert not just in the woodsman's

THE STRANGER DEFLECTED THE BLOW WITHOUT FLINCHING

arts but also in handling weapons of all kinds. Under his supervision, the recruits learned skills in archery and swordsmanship that they could never have imagined a few months before.

Thanks to Robin and Little John's teaching, the powerless peasants who had run to the forest were gradually transformed into capable fighting men. They learned to deflect sword thrusts to the chest with an upward sweep of the blade, and how to stop a bow from dipping at the crucial moment when the arrow is fired. They practiced wrestling holds, mastered camouflage tactics and learned ways of unhorsing riders using tree-branches. By the time spring had turned into full summer, they no longer looked the sad, ragged and demoralized group that had originally drifted into the woods. Now they were hardened forest-dwellers who were experts in the arts of self-defense.

Even so, Robin was always on the lookout for promising additions to the band. So his interest was roused when he heard about a monk who had taken up

residence on the fringes of the forest, and who was said to be unusually strong. The monk's name was Tuck, and it was said that he had left his monastery after a disagreement with the abbot over money that the establishment was paying to Prince John. Now he was living in a riverbank cave that served him as a hermitage. He earned money for his food by ferrying travelers across the stream.

As reports of the monk's strength continued to come in, Robin decided to pay him a visit.

"I can teach my men to look after their bodies well enough," he jokingly told Will Scarlett (as Will Scathlock now chose to be called), "but maybe I need a little help when it comes to their souls."

So, one midsummer afternoon Robin made his way to the riverbank opposite the friar's cell and shouted for the ferryman. A remarkable figure emerged from the cave. Friar Tuck was a strongly built man standing over six feet tall; but the size of his shoulders and chest was nothing compared to the majestic swell of his belly. Indeed, his spreading girth pushed out his robes so far that his legs rarely touched the cloth when he moved,

making it look as if he was gliding rather than walking over the ground.

The monk clambered into a small rowboat that sank dangerously close to the water level under his weight, and pulled his way rapidly over the stream. He stepped out to let Robin aboard, then with a few hefty pulls on the oars carried him safely over to the other side.

The boat reached the bank and the friar pointed a fat finger at a pile of coins lying on a mat nearby, reminding his passenger of the duty of charity as he did so. Robin, however, had come to test Tuck's character, so he stayed put on his seat.

"Forgive me, friar," he said with mock politeness, "but I'm afraid I've changed my mind. I've decided to go back the way I came. So would you be so kind as to row me across a second time?"

The big monk turned to face Robin. For an instant, it seemed as though he was going to say something to him ~ something unchristian. Then, mastering his feelings, he stepped back into the boat without a word. Picking up the oars once more, he propelled the craft back to the other bank.

This time Robin made as if to climb out before stopping and settling back in his place.

"You know, I think I've changed my mind again," he said. "I will go on after all. Take me back to the other side."

FRIAR TUCK WAS A STRONGLY BUILT MAN

The monk started to rise, but Robin tapped his sword hilt to discourage any rashness. In silence, Tuck picked up the oars and started rowing. He rowed the boat to midstream. Then, leaning forward as if for a particularly powerful stroke, he dropped the oars and seized his passenger's ankles instead. Before Robin knew what was happening, he was on his back in the bottom of the boat, where Tuck, grabbing Robin's tunic in one huge hand, lifted him up like so much unwanted ballast and dropped him unceremoniously overboard.

While Robin floundered in the water, the friar muttered a hasty prayer in Latin, seeking pardon for his transgression. He didn't get the chance to finish it, for his passenger, having managed to secure a footing on the river-bed, caught hold of the side of the boat and jerked it downward with such force that the craft turned over, hurling the friar into the water.

Friar Tuck came up roaring. But before he could fall on Robin as he meant to, he got distracted by a small fish caught wriggling in the collar of his habit ~ a sight so strange that it sent his intended victim into peals of laughter.

By the time Tuck had managed to remove the fish, he too had come to see the funny side of the situation, so when Robin stretched out a hand to him, he took it, resisting the urge to tug it mightily and send the stranger sprawling once more in the water.

"I owe you an explanation," Robin told him. "My name's Robin Hood. I'd heard how strong you were, and I wanted to see for myself if the stories were true. And I thought that while I was doing it I might as well find out a little about your courage, too." He gestured at the friar's wet robes with a dripping arm. "I think we're through when it comes to soaking each other," he added. "So why not come back with me to Sherwood?"

The friar seemed troubled by the offer. "I thought of coming to you when I first left the monastery," he said. "But then it struck me that life in the forest might not suit me "

"Why ever not?" Robin demanded. "We have everything you have here, and friendship besides. What put you off?"

The monk cast a glance down at his spreading belly, and the problem became clear.

"It's a hungry sort of life you lead there, I suppose?" he inquired mournfully.

"Not at all," Robin told him,

laughing. "There's venison and fruit of every kind, and we have friends outside who bring us joints of beef and pork and lamb to vary our diet. We store barrels of wine and beer, and..."

"I'll come," said Tuck without waiting to hear more. And so saying he returned with Robin to Sherwood. From that moment on the two men were the best of friends and never again had a reason to quarrel.

By this time, Robin and his followers, who at first had slept out under the stars, had set up a permanent camp in the heart of the forest. A couple of large caves provided the main refuges. The outlaws used them for storing food, and as dry places to sleep on stormy nights. To cover the entrances they constructed screens of leafy branches that so exactly matched the surrounding shrubbery that only a keen-eyed observer could spot them.

For shelter in finer weather, they hollowed tunnels in thickets where the twig and leaf cover was so dense that even the fiercest rainstorms hardly penetrated them. Protected from prying eyes, the men could sleep snug on straw pallets, with their weapons close at hand in case of attack.

The outlaws were now the masters of the forest, and no travelers could pass through Sherwood without being stopped and asked their business. Poor people were allowed to travel on unhindered; if they were very hard up, Robin's men would sometimes give them money or food to help them on their way.

The rich and powerful were not so lucky. Wealthy voyagers would be invited to eat with the outlaws. It was an invitation they could hardly refuse, for Robin's followers were well-armed; and after they had dined, Robin would demand half the money they carried with them as payment. The funds raised were sufficient to ensure that the band never went without, and there was cash left over to help the needy in the nearby villages.

By now Robin's men were held in such awe that they rarely had much trouble collecting the contributions. Most of the people that they stopped handed over their purses without any prompting. But every now and then they came across less obliging travelers. Even then, the outlaws rarely had to do more than show their weapons to get what they wanted.

One morning, however, two of the men limped back into camp bruised and bleeding. A third dragged in their attacker, securely bound. With many recriminations the trio recounted how the youth ~ a pageboy whose face was half hidden by a large cap ~ had drawn his sword when challenged and turned on them, even though he was outnumbered three to one. After overpowering him only with great difficulty, the three had brought him back to the camp for Robin to decide a fitting punishment.

Robin looked at the youth closely. There seemed something oddly familiar about the slim young figure. But it was only when the newcomer spoke, saying "Robin, don't you recognize me?", that he finally got an inkling of who it was. In disbelief, he reached forward and lifted off the page's cap. A cascade of chestnut-brown hair fell down. It was Marian, dressed up as a boy to escape the prying eyes of her father's guards as she made her way to Sherwood.

If Robin was taken aback at the discovery, the men who had struggled with her were even more astonished. But the resistance she had put up came as no surprise to Robin, who knew no one told Marian what to do unless she

chose to do it. He untied her hands and explained who she was to her captors, who looked so shamefaced at the explanation that Marian burst out laughing, setting everyone at ease again.

Marian brought news with her ~ bad news. Locksley Hall and its lands had been confiscated by Prince John after Robin's escape. Now they were to be given to Guy of Gisborne as a reward for his part in the outlawing.

And there was worse to come. Marian revealed that Guy had become a regular visitor at Arlingford Castle, where she lived with her father. From the looks he kept giving her and the compliments he paid her, she feared that he planned to win not just Robin's lands but his intended bride as well.

Robin was outraged. He could hardly be dissuaded from riding to Locksley there and then to confront his rival. It needed all Marian's tact and diplomacy to persuade him of the hopeless odds he would face if he challenged Guy in this way.

Eventually he calmed down enough to talk the situation through, and the two worked out a plan. Robin promised to be patient. He agreed that Marian should return to her father's castle before she was missed. She promised to get a message through to him by any means she could if danger threatened. Meanwhile, Robin was to find a way of getting his enemy to Sherwood. In the forest he was sure he would have the chance to get his revenge.

Marian got ready to go. Before she rode away, Robin took her hand and the two solemnly renewed their vows. In front of the assembled band, they swore to complete the interrupted marriage as soon as King Richard had returned and Robin was restored to his lands. Then Marian mounted her horse and rode out of the camp. Robin never felt sadder than he did at that moment, watching the lone figure riding away from him through the trees and knowing she was moving back into another life.

The Snatching of Will Scarlett

Robin needed to find out what was going on at Locksley Hall, even though Marian had persuaded him that it would be too dangerous to risk a visit. He wanted to  know if the servants who had served him faithfully ~ him and his father before him ~ would still have jobs under the new master. And what was to become of all his possessions?

Since he couldn't go himself without being recognized, he chose Will Scarlett to take his place. It was very dangerous work, not least because Will also risked being recognized at Locksley. But he could use his contacts there to find out more than any stranger could. Besides, he was eager to go; Will would have jumped at any chance to outwit the Sheriff.

To disguise himself, Will took off the scarlet tunic he usually wore and pulled on a peasant's smock. Then he knelt down and rubbed mud on his face and hands. When he stood up again, the others hardly knew him. He looked like a humble serf, back from working in the fields.

As Will was leaving, he heard someone call his name. He recognized the voice; it was Dickon, Much's son. As the youngest of Robin's band, Dickon had been waiting for a chance to show what he was worth. He wanted to come too. Will looked over to Robin, and Robin nodded. So Will and Dickon set off together through the forest.

It was five or six miles to Locksley, but it didn't take long to get there. Will knew all the short cuts and the woodsmen's paths. Soon they were at the forest's edge, looking out over the old manor where Robin's family had lived for so long. It was a sad sight now, as Robin's one-time servants milled around, trying to find out what would happen to them under their new master.

WILL AND DICKON SET OFF TOGETHER THROUGH THE FOREST

Hidden among the trees, Dickon watched as Will went to find out what was happening. The boy saw him walking up to one of the servants. The man looked at Will closely, but if he recognized him he was sensible enough not to show it; the Sheriff's men were nearby. The two talked for a moment, then Will moved away. Glancing around to check that no one was watching, he slipped back among the trees.

He told Dickon what he had learned. Guy of Gisborne was inside the building with a dozen of the Sheriff's men, among them the treacherous Wurman. They were questioning the servants one by one, to find out where their loyalties lay. A kind word about Robin was enough to lose a man his job; if he said more, he risked losing his head.

Will had noticed that there were no guards on the doors. Forgetting Robin's warnings to be careful, he had worked out a daring plan. He told Dickon to stay exactly where he was, then pulled his hood over his head and strode back to join the crowd. When he was sure no one was looking, he walked up to the door of the house and disappeared inside.

Dickon stood rooted to the spot, his eyes glued to the doorway. The minutes ticked by. At first everything seemed to be going well, but then suddenly there was a stir among the crowd and Will came flying out of the house. The Sheriff's men were at his heels.

Will headed for the trees where Dickon was waiting. He was a fast runner, and at first he managed to pull away from the men who were chasing him. But then Dickon saw two of them leaping onto horses that were tethered nearby. His heart sank; not even Will could outrun a mounted soldier.

Will reached the trees before the Sheriff's men could catch him. Dickon ran over to him. The panting man pulled a large leather bag from beneath his cloak and thrust it into his hands. "Get this to Robin!" he hissed, gazing wildly around for somewhere for Dickon to hide. His eyes fell on the hollow trunk of a damaged oak. "In there!" he cried, seizing Dickon by his waist and dropping him bodily into the cavity. Spiders and woodlice scattered as Dickon's legs scraped against the bark.

Dickon was still clutching the bag. Peeping inside, he saw something glittering. Jewels! And mixed in with them was the dull glow of gold. So that was why Will had gone into the house. Dickon gripped the bag tight. He realized that he had the Locksley family treasure in his hands.

There wasn't much time to worry about the treasure now though. The horsemen were in among the trees, and there was no way for Will to escape. From

his hiding place in the tree trunk, Dickon heard everything that followed: the pounding of the horses' hooves as the Sheriff's men closed in; the cry Will gave as they finally rode him down; his fierce denials when they called him a thief and a traitor. Then, as the rest of the men crashed into the thicket, Dickon heard a new voice. It was the whining tones of Wurman, identifying the captive as Will Scathlock, once Robert of Locksley's

steward and now one of Robin Hood's gang.

Dickon heard more too, and things he wished he hadn't. There was talk of Nottingham Castle where Will was to be taken ~ of the dungeons there, of the thumbscrew and the rack and other tortures that could make a strong man faint with pain. Then he learned the worst news of all. The next day at noon Will would be taken out to the castle green and hanged. That would be a lesson, the Sheriff's man said, to anyone else thinking of running off to join Robin Hood.

Dickon waited in the tree trunk until long after the horsemen had ridden off, dragging their prisoner behind them. He was shivering, not so much with cold as with fear at the terrible news he had to take back to the camp. When he was sure the coast was clear, he eased himself out of his hiding place. Then he made his way back through the forest as fast as he could.

When the hunters in Robin Hood's band heard rustling in the bushes nearby, they snatched up their bows, thinking a stray animal might be coming their way. Then they saw Dickon limping back into the glade. His cloak was torn, and his cheeks and legs were scratched by brambles. He was out of breath from running, and could hardly manage to stammer out the story he had to tell.

There were gasps of wonder when Dickon opened the leather bag and showed the outlaws the gold and jewels inside. When he had finished his tale, a babble of voices rose up as everyone pitched in with their own idea of how to free Will. Then Robin's voice rang out across the clearing. A hush fell as the others turned to hear what he had to say.

"Don't worry," he reassured them, his eyes darting across the crowd. "We'll find a way to get Will out. We owe him too much not to help him in his hour of need. We'll not leave him to be carrion for the Nottingham Castle crows."

The others murmured in agreement. "Let's storm the castle!" one voice cried from the back of the crowd. But Robin raised his hand, and silence fell again.

"We can't fight our way in," he said. "There'll be too many guards, and they'd murder Will before we could hope to reach him. But there are other ways to free

him." He looked around the crowd. "Does anyone here come from Nottingham?" he enquired. A dozen hands shot up. "Do any of you have friends among the Sheriff's men?" This time only three or four hands were raised. Robin waved those people aside. "We have things to talk over," he told them. "I have the makings of a plan... "

Early the next morning Robin set out through the forest with a dozen chosen helpers. Among them were two or three of the Nottingham folk he'd talked to the previous afternoon. Before they reached the gates of the town they separated. One of them ~ William of Goldsborough ~ had special instructions. He headed in the direction of the castle.

By then the town was wide awake, and the streets were bustling. There was a special stir in the air, for everyone had heard the news of Will Scarlett's capture and what would happen to him at noon. There were plenty of townspeople who were curious to see one of the Sherwood outlaws close up, particularly with the hangman waiting for him. But Will had friends in the town, too, who would have been glad enough to help him, given half a chance.

As midday drew near, a huge crowd gathered on the green before the castle gates. A wooden stage had been put up where a maypole had once stood, before King Richard had gone away. On the platform a solidly built wooden frame loomed against the sky. It was a gallows, and from its topmost beam the hangman's noose swung gently, waiting for another victim.

Guards ringed the platform, the sunlight glinting on their coats of mail. The sight of them was enough to make many people in the crowd mutter curses under their breath. But one man seemed happy enough to see them there. He was a stooped figure standing at the front of the crowd. He wore a travel-stained pilgrim's cloak, and even though his voice was old and cracked, he obviously liked the sound of it. He sang the praises of Prince John and the Sheriff to anyone who would listen, not seeming to notice the glares he got in return. In his opinion, not just Will Scarlet but all the Sherwood thieves should be strung up together.

A few minutes before noon, horses' hooves clattered in the narrow streets. People in the crowd strained to see who was coming. A dozen armed horsemen rode up to the green. Behind them came a horse-drawn wagon carrying a priest and two more soldiers. The fourth figure was a tall man with his hands tied behind his back. There was an awed murmur as the crowd recognized Will Scarlett.

The wagon drew up by the platform, and Will stepped out. There was no fear in his eyes ~ only anger when they fell on the Sheriff's men. But that was nothing to the hatred they showed when a second group of soldiers arrived, guarding a thin-lipped figure in an ermine-lined cape. It was the Sheriff himself, come to crow over his victim.

The Sheriff stepped forward to address the crowd, and silence fell. He told them that an accomplice of the bandit Robin Hood stood before them. "And," he went on, "you'll soon see what happens to all such creatures. Those who defy the law die by the law. People who break Prince John's peace must fall to the hangman at last." He turned to face the scaffold, ready to give the signal for the execution. It was only then he realized that something was wrong. One important element of a public hanging was missing: there was no hangman.

The Sheriff looked around angrily. Where could the wretch be? He waved the captain of the guard over, and the two men whispered together for a moment. Then, scowling thunderously, the Sheriff turned back to the crowd.

"Who has seen Luke Longshank?" he wanted to know. Silence. He tried again. "You all know our hangman," he said. "He's hanged enough criminals on this platform. So where is he? Who can tell me why he is not at his post?"

The crowd started to murmur. Will's friends glanced hopefully at one another ~ but not for long. A figure was shuffling towards the platform. It was the cloaked pilgrim from the front of the crowd.

"I know, your Honor," he croaked. "I can explain, your Worship."

Surprised, the Sheriff turned to listen. "He's had an accident, your Lordship," the man went on. "A fall from a horse. He can't move from his bed. So he sent me instead."

"You!" the Sheriff exclaimed in astonishment. "And what, pray,

THE HANGMAN AND HIS VICTIM LEAPED DOWN INTO THE CROWD

might you know about hanging?"

"There's not much I don't know, your Excellency," the man replied. "I was a hangman in old King Henry's days, before Prince John was even born. It was from me that Longshank learned his trade. I'm older now than I was, maybe, but I still have no love for thieves and bandits." He glared at Will Scarlett. "For two groats," he went on, "I'll be happy enough to send that one to his Maker."

The Sheriff looked doubtful. He turned again to the captain and there was another whispered conversation. Reluctantly, he turned back to the hooded figure. "You'll have your money," he said tersely.

The man needed no more encouragement. Bowing reverently to the Sheriff, he climbed onto the platform and moved around to the back of the condemned man. He leaned forward and seemed to whisper something in Scarlett's ear. Then suddenly he threw back his hood.

The head beneath was younger than anyone could have expected. The stoop had gone now, and the pilgrim seemed to grow taller before the crowd's gaze. Momentarily sunlight glinted on steel as the blade of a hunting knife cut through the prisoner's bonds. Then the pilgrim flung off his cloak. Beneath it, there was Lincoln green, the color that Robin Hood always wore. Moving like athletes, the hangman and his victim leaped together down into the crowd.

For a moment the spectators froze, paralyzed by shock. There were gasps as the words 'Robin Hood' echoed from mouth to mouth. Then a path opened up before the fugitives, only to close again as the Sheriff's guards clattered down the steps after them.

The soldiers didn't get far. A swarm of arrows stopped them in their tracks. Following Robin's lead, a dozen other outlaws scattered among the crowd had thrown off their cloaks to reveal longbows strung ready for action. While the Sheriff's men cowered behind their shields, Robin and Will ran to untether the guards' own horses.

Soon the other bowmen had joined them, and the whole band was thundering through the streets of Nottingham on their enemies' mounts, heading for the safety of Sherwood. Behind them they could hear the Sheriff screaming insults as his men stumbled around vainly, helpless without their horses.

That evening there was feasting in the forest far into the night, and nobody enjoyed it more than the twelve heroes of the Nottingham raid. Or rather, than eleven of them. The twelfth, William of Goldsborough, had gone that morning to invite his one-time neighbor, Luke Longshank, to drink to old times together. And drink they did, long and hard ~ long enough to keep Luke away from the scaffold where he was supposed to be hanging Will Scarlett. So, while the rest of the band were making merry, William lay fast asleep under the stars. He'd done enough celebrating to last him for a very long time.

PAYING BACK DEBTS

One day some of Robin's men came across a lone traveler riding through the forest. They could see from the sword that swung by his side that he was a knight. But he was plodding  along slowly with his head bowed, not strutting proudly as knights usually did. In fact he looked so wretched that the outlaws were tempted to let him go on his way without stopping him. But their curiosity got the better of them, so they hailed him and asked him what he was doing in Sherwood.

Most people, seeing Robin's men in their path, were either scared or angry, but the knight seemed neither. He just gazed at them blankly, as if he didn't care what they did with him. He raised no objection when they asked him to ride with them to meet Robin Hood.

Robin greeted the knight hospitably, as he did all travelers not in the service of the Sheriff of Nottingham. There was a wrestling match in progress, with Little John comfortably beating all comers. Robin invited the stranger to watch the fun, and made sure that he had plenty of ale to refresh him.

Warmed by his welcome, the cloud that seemed to hang over the knight gradually lifted. By the time Little John had run out of challengers, he had relaxed enough to tell Robin the problem that was weighing on his mind.

His name, he said, was Sir Richard of Leigh, and he owned lands north of Sherwood. He had a son who, having gone off on a Crusade with King Richard, had been wounded in battle and taken prisoner. As was customary, his captors had demanded a ransom to release him. They wanted the huge sum of one thousand pounds ~ almost as much as Sir Richard's entire estate was worth. Yet if he could not find the money, he knew his son would be killed.

HE WAS PLODDING ALONG SLOWLY WITH HIS HEAD BOWED

By selling off land and valuables, the knight had managed to raise six hundred pounds. Despairing of finding the rest in time, he had turned to the Church to borrow the missing four hundred pounds. The man he had gone to was the Abbot of St. Mary's, the richest monastery in the district.

The Abbot ~ a grasping man who had long hankered after Sir Richard's estate ~ had agreed to lend the amount, but at a price. His terms were that the knight must pay every penny back within a year. If he failed to do so, he would have to hand everything he owned over to the monastery.

Sir Richard had had little choice but to accept. While the ransom was on its way to the Holy Land ~ a journey of many months ~ he set about raising funds as best he could to pay back the debt and save his castle and lands. It was a hard struggle, but in time he managed, with the help of friends, to gather almost the entire sum. With a few days to go he was only six pounds short, and was almost certain that he would be able to make up the rest.

Then disaster had struck. Just forty-eight hours before the year was up and the loan had to be repaid, a party of armed horsemen had ridden up to his castle. They were escorting tax collectors who proceeded to demand on the spot three hundred pounds which they claimed were owing to Prince John. Sir Richard did his best to explain the situation he was in, but the tax collectors would not listen. They insisted on taking the money away with them, and the armed men were there to see that they got it.

Sir Richard was devastated by the blow, which had fallen just the day before his meeting with Robin. He knew there was no hope of making up the sum, or even of repaying the friends who had come to his aid. The chief of the escort had told him the soldiers had been sent by the Sheriff of Nottingham, and since he had nothing better to do, he had decided to ride to

Nottingham and throw himself on the Sheriff's mercy. He intended to appeal to him to return the money, in exchange for a promise to pay it back in stages over the months to come.

Robin shook his head sadly when the knight had finished.

"You'll get no help from the Sheriff," he said. "Most likely he's in league with the Abbot. The two are thick as thieves," he added bitterly.

The knight put his head in his hands.

"Then there's no hope," he said.

Robin sat thinking. He'd been touched by the story, for it wasn't long since he'd lost his own home to Guy of Gisborne. Suddenly he looked over to the knight. There was a glimmer of hope in his eyes.

"Have the tax collectors gone back to Nottingham yet?" he asked.

"I don't think so," the knight replied. "They had one more call to make first. They were planning to go to Thoresby this morning."

"Thoresby!" Robin slapped his knee, and a smile spread across his face. "In that case I think we might just be able to help you," he said. "If I'm right, they should be heading back toward Nottingham this afternoon ~ through Sherwood Forest."

Robin already had a plan in mind. He was on his feet now, muttering as he worked out the details and shouting orders once he had them settled. At his bidding the whole camp sprang to life. Men snatched up weapons and ran for their horses. Meanwhile, at Robin's request, Will Scarlett headed for the cave where the stores were kept. There he found shovels, a large joint of meat, and reels of bowstring.

Within minutes the whole band was on the move toward the road by which the Sheriff's men would have to pass. It was a wide track lined by clumps of bushes. The thickets alternated with clearer stretches where there was little vegetation. Robin chose a spot where there was good cover on one side of the road; on the other a clearing opened out behind a thin screen of trees. He smiled contentedly. It suited his purposes exactly.

He reckoned he had a couple of hours to spare before the Sheriff's men arrived, but to be safe he sent a couple of horsemen down the road to keep watch. Then he set some of the band to digging a trench across the road and gathering twigs and branches. When the trench was about waist-deep, Robin had it loosely filled with the branches. Most of the earth from the trench had been dumped out of sight, but Robin had kept just enough to cover the twigs and branches. By the time the surface had been leveled off, the hole was virtually impossible to spot.

Meanwhile, other men had been busy in the trees that screened the clearing, running bowstring ~ strong as steel, and almost invisible in the shade ~ from trunk to trunk at a mounted man's height. Once they had finished, Robin himself carefully positioned the joint of meat within the clearing, in clear sight of the road.

Now Robin told the outlaws to take cover. Some hid in the undergrowth around the clearing; others took up position high in the trees, looking down on the road beneath them. The men waited. In the silence, birdsong filled the air. Then came the clatter of pounding hooves. It was Robin's guards, returning to say that the Sheriff's men were on the way.

All was quiet again as the soldiers approached. There were a dozen of them, clad in chain mail and with heavy swords brushing their mounts' flanks. They were escorting a farmcart drawn by a couple of draught horses. The tax collectors sat on the wagon, guarding a heavy metal chest.

Suddenly there was a shout from one of the soldiers. He had spotted a lone figure in Lincoln green crouching in the glade. The man was hacking at the meat with a hunting knife. His bow and arrow lay by his side.

"Poacher!" the leader of the escort shouted to his men. "Seize him!" The soldiers in front of the wagon peeled away to ride the law-breaker down. The crouching man leaped to his feet and ran off into the wood. But his pursuers didn't get far. As they charged through the screen of trees, the bowstrings stretched between the trunks caught them and sent them tumbling like bowling pins. Robin's men swarmed out of their hiding places and attacked them as they floundered on the forest floor.

The rest of the escort turned to ride to their aid. But just at that moment there were whinnies of alarm from the horses pulling the wagon. Reaching the trench, they felt the ground sagging under their hooves. In fact the branches were firm enough for them to scramble over. But they would not take the weight of the wagon. The front wheels sank in up to the axle, bringing the whole convoy to a shuddering halt.

This was the moment the bowmen in the trees had been waiting for. A hail of arrows rained down on the soldiers. As they wheeled uncertainly, looking for somewhere to take cover, they got another nasty

surprise. The outlaws hidden in the undergrowth rose up with fearful yells and fell upon them. It was the last straw. Clapping spurs to their mounts, they took off down the road to Nottingham like startled rabbits, leaving nothing but a cloud of dust behind them.

Robin's men stripped the captured soldiers of their armor and weapons, leaving them shivering in their short tunics. Then they freed them to run back to Nottingham after their comrades. The tax collectors had already slipped away, so the victory was complete. Robin and his men could now examine the wagon's load at leisure. The chest was locked, and for extra security had been bound with rope, with wax seals on the knots.

The bonds were quickly cut through, and Robin managed to force the lock with his dagger. The heavy lid creaked open. There were whistles of amazement when the outlaws saw what was inside. The chest contained a treasure in gold coins extorted from across the district. Sir Richard's three hundred pounds made up only a small part of the haul.

The outlaws carried the booty back to their base in the forest. A feast was prepared there under Friar Tuck's supervision. The band ate and drank their fill, and shared many toasts to King Richard and the crusaders. Then Robin gave Sir Richard not just the three hundred pounds the tax collectors had taken but enough to cover the entire ransom. Even so, there was still money left over to refill the outlaws' own coffers.

The next day the Abbot of St. Mary's, who knew nothing of what had happened in the forest, was contemplating the improvements he would make to Sir Richard's lands, when a visitor was announced. It was the knight himself, poorly dressed in a threadbare cloak and wearing a forlorn expression. The mere sight of him cheered up the Abbot, who now felt sure of getting what he wanted.

"Well, Sir Richard?" the Abbot asked, rubbing his hands expectantly, "Have you brought the money you owe me?"

"Can I ask you a question first?" the knight responded dolefully. "I've done everything in my power to raise the money. Would you be prepared to extend the time for repayment?"

The Abbot feigned concern, though it wasn't easy for him to hide the satisfaction he felt at seeing his plans work out so well.

"Personally speaking, there's nothing I'd like more," he said insincerely. "Speaking as a man of God, that is. But I have other responsibilities, you know. I have obligations, duties to my abbey. No, I'm afraid I couldn't consider it. The money must be paid."

"Not even in the name of Christian charity?" Sir Richard asked hopefully.

"Don't talk to me about charity," the Abbot snapped, impatient now to have the matter settled. "You were glad enough to take the loan when it was offered, and you promised to repay it by today. If you don't have the money I want the deeds to your lands. That was the arrangement, and I need them now."

"So you wouldn't consider a delay?" Sir Richard asked again, this time in a grimmer, less pleading tone of voice.

"Delay?" The very idea was enough to infuriate the Abbot. "No, I wouldn't. There'll be no delay, not for a day and not for an hour. You've taken up enough of my time already, you pauper. Give me what you owe me and get out!"

Suddenly Sir Richard, who had entered the room bent and stooping, raised himself to his full height.

"Then I'll waste no more of your precious time," he replied angrily. "If I've kept you longer than necessary, it was only to find out something ~ something about you. I wanted to learn if money mattered more to you than charity. And I think we've both seen the answer."

So saying, he reached inside his cloak and pulled out two brimming moneybags. "Take your money," he added contemptuously, throwing the bags down on the table in front of him.

There, before the lender's startled eyes, he carefully counted out every penny that he owed. He pushed the coins over to the Abbot, who was still sitting open-mouthed. Then he gathered together the rest of the money and put it back beneath his cloak.

"I've learned plenty from this meeting," he said before he turned to go, "and there are a couple of things you could learn from it too. One is not to judge people by appearances. The other is that thinking about your property a little less and practicing charity a little more might make you a better Abbot. And a better man."

So saying, he strode out of the door, leaving his adversary, who had not moved from his seat, still too stunned by the turn events had taken even to react in any way. The Abbot of St. Mary's was renowned throughout Nottinghamshire for his silver tongue, which had made him what he was. But for once in his life, the smooth-talking churchman discovered that he couldn't find a word to say.

MARIAN IN DANGER

Things had not been going well for Marian since her visit to Sherwood. Guy of Gisborne had become a regular visitor at Arlingford Castle, and he seemed to have more

of a hold than ever over her father. All Lord Fitzwalter's hopes for Marian were now apparently centered on the man she most detested.

She was given no peace. At breakfast her father would tell her how handsome Guy was. Over lunch she'd have to listen while he outlined the prospects Guy could offer her. And at dinner, more than likely, there would be Guy himself, simpering at her across the dining hall. Whenever he spoke to her, she had to fight back an urge to pour the contents of her wine goblet over him ~ or at the very least to kick him in the shins.

The worst thing of all was that she couldn't say what she felt, for her father thought that any word against Guy was nothing less than disrespect toward himself. Lord Fitzwalter was a stubborn old man with a hot temper, and he was used to having his own way.

"Lord save us," he'd shout if she dared breathe a word of complaint, "Was ever a father so troubled by his children?" And Marian would bite her lip and fall silent again, nursing her resentment in secret.

Matters finally came to a head one morning when her father strode unexpectedly into her room to announce that a visitor was coming to the castle. The Bishop of Hereford, newly appointed by Prince John, was traveling to Nottingham to visit the Sheriff; the two men knew each other, it seemed, as fellow members of the Prince's circle. Even though no one at Arlingford had met the Bishop, he planned to break his journey there because it was conveniently located on his route, just a day's ride from the city.

Marian was amazed. Guests were rare enough at Arlingford at the best of times. She couldn't see why, when her father did decide to receive one, it had to be a total stranger, and a favorite of Prince John's at that. Unfortunately for her, she couldn't stop herself from saying so.

"The Bishop is an important man, and he has powerful friends," her father told her irritably. "People like that must be treated with respect." Then he stopped and smiled at her condescendingly. "But how could you understand these matters? You're just a girl, and these are men's affairs."

Now, if there was one thing that made Marian really angry, it was being told that she didn't understand things when she did, only too well. So when her father went on to say that Guy of Gisborne was coming that afternoon and he expected her to receive him politely, she did something she had never done before. Quietly, she said that she wouldn't.

"You shall wait at the gatehouse to greet him," her father continued, pretending not to have heard, "and then escort him to the great hall."

"I will not," Marian repeated, louder this time.

"You will wear your finest tunic and surcoat," her father went on, with a warning note of anger in his voice. "And it may amuse him to hear you play the lute before we sit down to dinner."

Marian walked over to the old man and looked him straight in the eyes.

"I will not receive Guy of Gisborne," she said. "I will not even enter the same room as him. And if you force me to, I shall neither speak to him nor look at him, so help me God."

Lord Fitzwalter's mouth dropped, and for a second he stood gasping for air. Then a strange puce color spread over his face as the full impact of what he had just heard dawned on him. In all his life, no one had ever dared oppose him so openly. And this was from his own daughter!

When he finally found his tongue, all he managed to say was: "You'll come to regret those words, my girl." Then he stalked out of the room, slamming the door and leaving Marian to wonder what punishment lay in store for her.

She found out later the same day. She was to be locked in her room until she agreed to apologize and to receive Guy in the way her father wished. Until then she was to see no one except a maid-servant, who would bring her food at mealtimes.

Imprisoned in her chamber, Marian came close to despair. She knew the only person who could help her was Robin, but she couldn't think of any way to let him know what had happened. Her only contact was the maid, who was far too terrified of Lord Fitzwalter to risk helping his daughter.

Marian was sitting in her room staring glumly at the embroidery frame that stood unused in one corner when suddenly she had a flash of inspiration. The next time the maid came to the room, she was astonished to find Marian busy sewing. It was something she had never shown much interest in before, but now she started giving up most of the daylight hours to it.

Lord Fitzwalter was pleased to hear that his daughter had taken up such a suitable occupation. He was positively delighted when, one morning, the maid brought for his inspection a small, neatly-stitched panel. The words "SERVA ME" ~ Latin for "Save my Soul" ~ were picked out in red, bordered by a pattern of coats of arms and crosses.

Here at last, Lord Fitzwalter thought, was a sign that his daughter was repenting her wickedness. So he was only too happy to give his permission when Marian asked if she could give the panel to a church to be displayed. And he raised no objection when she chose the chapel on the Locksley estate where she and

IMPRISONED IN HER CHAMBER, MARIAN CAME CLOSE TO DESPAIR

Robin had come so close to being married.

That was his mistake. For the vicar there was a good friend to both Robin and Marian, and as soon as he saw the panel he realized something was wrong. For "SERVA ME", as he well knew, could mean "Help Me" as well as "Save my Soul"; and to make the message plainer, Marian had sewn into the border the arms of the hated Guy of Gisborne.

The vicar soon got word to Robin, as Marian had hoped he would. And Robin wasted no time in using his contacts at the castle to find out what had happened. He also learned about the Bishop of Hereford's visit. Putting the two pieces of information together gave him an idea. He suddenly saw a way both to save Marian and humiliate a favorite of Prince John's.

A few days later the Bishop, accompanied by several monks and an escort of soldiers, was riding through Sherwood to Arlingford when the party was halted by the sight of a lone man sprawled across the path.

"Make way for the Bishop of Hereford!" the leader of the escort shouted. The man remained where he was. The chief waved two of his soldiers forward to investigate. They rode up to the man, who gestured at his leg and groaned. It looked as though he must have broken it. The soldiers rode back to report what they had found. The bishop snorted irritably.

"Get him out of the way," he told them. "We can send help when we reach Arlingford."

The guards dismounted and went to move the injured man. But before they could reach him, to their amazement he leaped to his feet and sprinted off into the forest. They never got a chance to chase him. Robin's men, who had been hiding at the side of the track, now rushed forward to attack the bishop's party. The ambushers had the advantage of surprise, and the skirmish that followed turned out to be no contest. Within minutes all the guards had been disarmed and the churchmen were on their knees, begging for mercy.

"You have nothing to fear from us," a voice told them from the undergrowth. Robin emerged from the trees. His sword was drawn but he was smiling politely. "We very rarely receive such distinguished visitors here in Sherwood," he told them. "We couldn't let company like yours pass unnoticed. You are our guests, and a banquet has been laid out in your honor. I trust you'll find our forest hospitality to your liking."

And so saying, he and his men led the Bishop, the monks and the disarmed soldiers off to a nearby clearing where a feast of venison had been prepared. It was a tempting sight, but just in case any of the visitors didn't want to stay for it, a ring of armed men had been posted around the clearing.

Under the circumstances, no one turned down the outlaw's invitation. And Robin saw his guests were well looked after. The food was excellent and the drink flowed freely. By the end of the meal, several of the monks had decided that the company of outlaws wasn't nearly as bad as it was generally thought to be.

That was when Robin sprang a surprise upon the visitors. He told the churchmen that his men needed to borrow their robes. It wouldn't be for long, he promised, and they would have comfortable tunics to wear in exchange. The Bishop started to protest, but the sight of the armed men all around soon stopped him. He watched sullenly while his monks were led away to slip off their habits.

Finally he had to put up with the indignity of surrendering his own magnificent purple robes. In return he was given a plain woodsman's tunic.

Friar Tuck, who had overseen the preparation of the feast, now vanished from the glade. When he came back a few minutes later he was wearing the purple vestments. There was an awed silence as he made his way over to Robin. Seeing him in the robes, with a miter on his head and a staff in his hand, even the most hardened outlaw had to admit he looked every inch a bishop. In a stately manner he mounted the bishop's own horse and set off for Arlingford in his place. A couple of Robin's men dressed as monks rode with him.

If Tuck was nervous as he approached the castle, he didn't show it. He had taken on a bishop's dignity along with the vestments, and when the gates swung open before him, he rode in as majestically as if he'd been born to the cloth. Lord Fitzwalter greeted him with the respect due to a senior churchman and a friend of the Sheriff. But he couldn't help showing his surprise that so important a man had chosen to travel with so few companions.

Tuck swiftly explained that the soldiers who had escorted him through Sherwood had stayed behind to check the neighborhood for any signs of the notorious villain Robin Hood. His host was happy to accept the explanation, secretly thanking his stars that there wouldn't be as many mouths to feed as he had feared.

At dinner that evening, the Friar did his best to make up for the missing men, eating enough for any three normal people. Only after he had done full justice to the labors of the castle cooks did he steer the conversation around to Marian.

"Our one regret in so pleasant an evening is not to have met your daughter," he told his host. "Word of the beauty and wit of the Lady Marian has even reached us in Hereford. We had hoped to meet her at dinner to see if her reputation was not outshone by the reality."

Lord Fitzwalter sighed. "She should indeed have been here to meet you," he agreed. "But the girl is as stubborn as she is bright and as strong-willed as she is beautiful. She deliberately flouted my wishes. I had no choice but to punish her for her behavior." And then, with a little encouragement from his guest, he went on to tell the whole story of her disobedience in the matter of Guy of Gisborne and the way in which he had chosen to discipline her.

The friar pretended to be sympathetic. "Strong-headed children need a firm hand," he agreed, nodding wisely. "But by now the Lord might have softened her heart and made her ready to see reason. Perhaps she would benefit from the help of a spiritual advisor. If I could be of use, I should be more than happy to offer my services."

At first Lord Fitzwalter declined the offer, but the churchman was so insistent that he gradually gave way. At heart he was flattered that such an important person should take an interest in his family problems. Eventually he agreed that the bishop should have a private talk with Marian that very evening to try to persuade her to mend her ways. He sent a servant upstairs to prepare her for the visit. Not many minutes later, Tuck was shown up to her room. The retainer who accompanied him handed him the key, asking him to lock the door and return it to the guard below at the end of the talk.

Tuck entered the room. At first he could not see Marian, who sat slumped in a chair near the fireplace, refusing even to acknowledge his presence.

"Peace be with you," he intoned. There was no response. He tried again. "My daughter..." he said in a kindly tone. Still silence. Then he hissed, "Marian, it's me!" and this time she looked over quickly enough. But, having only met the friar once before in Robin's camp, she failed to recognize him in his bishop's robes. She fell back despondently into her seat, determined not to say a word to any friend of the Sheriff's.

"Look at me, Marian. Don't you know me?" he whispered again. She turned toward him and examined him closely. Suddenly a glimmer of recognition crossed her face.

"But how will I ever get past the guards?" she wanted to know when she had finally accepted that it really was Tuck and he was there to rescue her. The friar winked knowingly. Then he reached inside his ample vestments and with a flourish produced a crumpled bundle. It was a spare monk's habit. Tuck gave it to her to pull over the clothes that she was wearing.

With the hood pulled up over her flowing brown hair, Marian looked the part well enough ~ sufficiently at any rate to fool the castle guards in the darkness. She was impatient to leave at once, but the friar insisted they wait a little longer.

He had arranged to meet his two companions in the courtyard in an hour's time, knowing that by then most of the castle would be asleep.

＊＊＊＊＊＊＊＊＊＊＊＊＊＊＊

When the time came, the two left the room, taking care to lock the door behind them. The guard who took the key had expected the bishop to be on his own, but didn't find anything odd in him having a monk with him.

Outside all was quiet, as the friar had reckoned. It was a dark night, and it wasn't easy for the two to find their way through the gloom to the stables where they were to meet their companions. A sudden burst of whinnying helped them get their bearings. They arrived to find the two outlaws waiting with the horses already saddled.

There was a slight delay when Marian insisted on fetching her own much-loved stallion, Aspen, who neighed softly with pleasure at the sound of his owner's footsteps. In a minute he too was saddled up, and the four figures, all in their ankle-length robes, were leading their mounts as quietly as possible across the deserted courtyard.

By now the moon was out, and their shadows moved ahead of them as they tiptoed cautiously past the castle buildings. Reaching the gatehouse, they found the doors fastened against them. Lifting the bar was easy enough, but outside an unpleasant surprise was waiting. The portcullis was down, and a quick examination soon showed that the machinery for opening it lay inside the locked gatehouse.

There was only one thing to do. Friar Tuck dismounted. He put on his miter and took up the bishop's staff to make himself look all the more impressive. Then he stepped up to the gatehouse and knocked on the door. There was no answer. He rapped again, slightly louder. Still no response. Finally he hammered on the door with all his might; and after a few seconds stirrings could be heard inside, and an irritable-looking man stuck his head out of an upstairs window and asked what the matter was.

"I am the Bishop of Hereford," said Friar Tuck in his most commanding tone, "and I must leave the castle now. I have been summoned away unexpectedly, on urgent spiritual business."

The man scratched his head, perplexed. He seemed to be in two minds. Eventually he said, "Well, I have my orders. I'm never to open the gates after dark. Not without my Lord's permission."

"Very well, then," said the friar calmly. "The two of us shall go and speak to Lord Fitzwalter together."

The head disappeared. The four companions exchanged nervous glances. A few seconds later the man emerged, with a cloak pulled hastily over his nightgown.

Finding himself face to face with the Bishop in his full regalia, the man bowed his head reverently. It was exactly what Tuck had hoped for. Raising his eyes heavenward, he muttered beseechingly, "Lord, have mercy on me, a sinner". Then he brought the staff down with considerable force on the gatekeeper's head, laying him out with one blow.

Tuck quickly bent down to see how much harm he'd done. When he'd convinced himself that the man had merely been knocked out and would have nothing worse than a bad bump to remember him by the next morning, he dragged him back into the gatehouse. Then he and the other outlaws together pulled up the portcullis ~ all that now stood between them and freedom.

They strained at the ropes, jumping nervously at every creak of the rusty machinery, then hurried back to the horses, locking the door behind them on the way. Even if the gatekeeper came to, they reckoned he probably wouldn't be able to make enough noise to wake the people in the castle until morning.

Even so, the four weren't taking any chances. Once they were clear of the gatehouse, they set off as fast as they could gallop for the safety of Sherwood. And none rode more swiftly than Marian, who was thrilled to realize her captivity was finally over.

They arrived in the small hours, to find the feast long over and the real Bishop and his party snoring dismally among the remnants. At the sound of horses, Robin, who'd been unable to sleep due to worrying about Marian, leaped to his feet. The two greeted each other joyfully.

Only one task now remained, and that was to get rid of the unwanted guests. The outlaws waited until first light. Then they woke the groaning men, their heads still heavy from the previous evening's feasting, and gave them back their clothes.

With their hands tied behind their backs, monks and soldiers alike were led through the forest to the track where they had first encountered Robin and his men. There they were lifted onto their horses ~ only facing backward, so they had to hang onto the pommels of their saddles as best they could to avoid falling off.

As the Bishop and his men shivered in the early-morning cold, Robin politely wished them goodbye. He told them he had removed the moneybags they had been carrying with them, but pointed out that this was no more than fair payment for the excellent dinner they had enjoyed the previous evening. Then, telling the Bishop to be sure to send his regards to the Sheriff, he slapped the flank of his horse and shooed it off.

And the last he saw of the Bishop and his party was the sight of a dozen sad-looking individuals clinging with bound hands onto their saddles as they trotted backward toward Nottingham.

The Final Challenge Part 1:
The Silver Arrow

One day exciting news reached Sherwood. There was to be an archery contest in Nottingham, at the city's famous Goose Fair. The best bowmen from all over the region were expected to compete against one another. And the prize was to be the famous Silver Arrow, handed down over the generations to the finest archer of the day.

The contest, which was open to all comers, was to be judged by the Sheriff of Nottingham himself. Robin knew that he shouldn't even think of going, and all the other outlaws told him he would be crazy to take the risk. But he also knew it was the kind of challenge he could never refuse. For he was sure that he was good enough to win the Silver Arrow.

Obviously, the only way he could compete was to go in disguise. He chose the part of a weather-beaten old crusader, just back from the Holy Land; that way, it would be easier to explain to the other archers why they'd never seen him before at contests.

To make his face look sunburned, he decided to rub red earth into it. He found a faded cloak and tunic, and hacked away with his sword at an old coat of mail until it had all the dents and scrapes of armor that had been through the wars. And he practiced speaking in a deeper voice than usual, embellishing his conversation with the foreign words and special slang that crusaders picked up on their travels.

Eventually he felt ready to try out the disguise. He left the rest of the band one morning, put on the crusader outfit, scrubbed his face with earth until it looked raw, and then set off on his own through the forest. Before long he was spotted by one of the outlaws. As he expected, the man called to him to stop. It was William of

Goldsborough, who had been with the band since the early days when Robin was still Robert of Locksley.

"What's your business in the forest?" William asked roughly. Robin said nothing. William came closer. For a moment Robin thought that he'd seen through the disguise, but then William said, "Well, what brings you here? Speak up," and he realized that he hadn't been recognized.

"Oi be one of Lionheart's men, back from the wars. The San'Terre we calls it, but it'ud be the Holy Land to the loikes uv you," Robin said. The accent sounded pretty unconvincing to him, but William seemed to accept it.

"In that case you'd better come and meet my master, Robin Hood," William told him. "If you're Lionheart's man, he'll be pleased..." But he never got the chance to finish. The stranger, dropping the false accent, told him that he *was* Robin, and William gasped in amazement.

The disguise had been such a success that Robin felt no further doubts about going to Nottingham. The only precaution he took was to ask Will Scarlett and Little John to make their own way to the Goose Fair. If he did run into difficulty, he thought he might need their help to get out of it.

The day of the fair dawned bright, and Robin set off for town early. Yet by the time he arrived, the streets were already packed.

Peddlers selling trinkets jostled alongside beggars asking for alms. Troupes of actors performed plays on improvised stages. Minstrels sang ballads to the strumming of lutes. Showmen tried to tempt customers into tents where, they promised, for a few pennies they'd see all the latest wonders brought back from the Holy Land.

The archery tournament was to be held on the green outside the castle. Wooden stands had been set up for the noble guests to watch in comfort; the other spectators had to stand in the open. In the center was a raised platform where the Sheriff himself was to sit.

News of the contest had spread far and wide, and Robin found that several hundred men had put their names down for it. There were so many of them that the elimination rounds had already started by the time he arrived. Anyone who failed to hit the target at fifty paces was at once excluded.

Robin had no trouble hitting the mark at that distance, nor when it was later moved to one hundred paces. But many of the other contestants did, and by the time the range was one hundred and fifty paces, the total number of competitors had been brought down to just forty-five.

By then it was midmorning, and the green was crowded with spectators. Before the final rounds of the contest started, soldiers rode up and cleared a path for the Sheriff, who arrived with his guests and took his place on the platform. When he gave the signal, the first of the forty-five stepped up to take aim.

Watching his rivals, Robin quickly realized that there were only two who came close to matching his skill. One was a tall, gaunt forester from Norfolk who rarely answered questions with more than a single word. The other was a soldier ~ a captain in the Sheriff's guard.

After a first round with the target at one hundred and fifty paces, the twenty-five archers whose arrows were farthest from the bull's-eye were knocked out of the competition. A second volley of arrows reduced the number to ten. With each shot, the captain and the forester were hitting the bull's-eye ~ but so was Robin.

Next the target was moved to two hundred paces, and the other competitors soon fell away. By now the crowd was starting to take sides. Each time the forester or the old crusader struck home, a cry went up from their supporters. But for the captain there was only light applause, for everybody knew that he was the Sheriff's man.

Finally only the three contenders were left, and a herald announced that the next round would be the last. Whoever's shot was closest to the center of the target would win the Silver Arrow.

The forester fired first. He'd been regularly hitting the bull's-eye, but now nervousness caused him to snatch a little at the bowstring as he loosed his shot. The arrow thudded into the white ring circling the bull's-eye. His supporters groaned in disappointment.

The captain stepped forward next. He was a big man, and he took forever to aim his bow. The crowd held its breath. But when he finally released the arrow, it sped unerringly to the very middle of the bull.

The Sheriff, who had been leaning forward tensely in his seat, now sat back, turning to his companions with a smile. He obviously thought the contest was as good as won. But Robin had still to shoot, and now he moved up to the line.

To start with he raised his bow so it was pointing well above the target. Even when he pulled it down he was still holding it loosely, letting it waver visibly in his hands until he had settled. He waited with the arrow poised until he knew he was completely relaxed. Then he sighted along the shaft and his left arm went rigid as steel. The crowd was so quiet that even the farthest spectators could hear the whoosh the arrow made as it soared from the bow.

It seemed a long time before it reached its mark. When it did, there was a small explosion of feathers and splinters, and for a split second no one could work out exactly what had happened. Then a startled gasp went up as the spectators realized that Robin's arrow had split the captain's shaft down the middle. The contest had ended in a tie.

All eyes turned on the Sheriff. He was scowling furiously, angry at seeing his champion's shot matched. Rising to his feet, he gave orders for the two winning contestants to approach the stands. He looked at the old crusader closely for several seconds, and Robin began to fear that his enemy had seen through his disguise. But the Sheriff only shook his

head irritably and said, "We need one winner, not two. Set a stick of wood at three hundred paces."

A buzz of excitement spread through the crowd as his men knocked a thin stick into the ground in front of the stands. Then they paced out the distance the archers would have to shoot from. The range seemed vast. By the time the Sheriff's man, who was shooting first, had made his way back to the line and taken aim, he looked a small and faraway figure to the waiting crowd.

The arrow sped through the air, and the spectators strained forward to see if it would strike home. The stick swayed as the arrow shot past, but when the judges examined it they found it unmarked. It was a close call, but the captain had missed. A sigh of relief went up from the crowd.

Now everyone was looking at the old crusader. As he waited to compose himself once more, he looked too old and frail to fire as far as the target, let alone hit it. But when the shaft was released, it flew straight and true. The stick split in two as the arrow sliced through its center.

HE SIGHTED ALONG THE SHAFT AND HIS LEFT ARM WENT RIGID AS STEEL

A roar of joy went up from the crowd. Some of the younger onlookers burst through the barriers and ran the length of the range to mob their hero. He was the people's champion now, and they hoisted him onto their shoulders to carry him in triumph to collect the trophy.

There was no rejoicing, though, among the Sheriff's friends. A line of soldiers stood guarding them, and as the crowd moved forward the soldiers' commander ordered his men to draw their swords. But the Sheriff, fearing a direct confrontation, signaled to them to sheathe them again. Then he called the commander over. The two men muttered together for a few seconds. Then the commander, gesturing to his men, slipped away behind the stand. Several soldiers followed him.

The green was still echoing to the cheers of the crowd when Robin's supporters reached the platform. They set their champion down at the foot of the stairs. The Sheriff had risen to his feet again and was standing waiting. Robin turned to wave to the crowd, then climbed the steps to claim his prize.

He was never to receive it. As he reached the top of the steps, the planks gave way. Feeling himself falling, he dropped his bow and grasped desperately for something to hold on to. There was nothing. Helpless, he felt himself dropping into blackness.

He landed heavily, twisting his ankle as he did so. Armed men were waiting for him, and his arms and legs were seized and quickly bound before he could do anything to defend himself. A gag was forced into his mouth, making it hard for him to breathe.

Somewhere far above him he could hear his supporters' cries of surprise and anger. But already the noise seemed far away. In the

darkness, he was dimly aware of shouting and the clashing of steel as the guards restored order. Then there was only a confused hubbub as people argued about the extraordinary event they had just witnessed.

Up close there was only the heavy breathing of the soldiers, and their leader's sneering voice: "Did you really think that you could fool the Sheriff?" he asked. "Didn't you realize we knew you'd come? And all we needed to capture the great Robin Hood was a simple trapdoor!"

Trussed up like a chicken, Robin was carried out to the back of the stands. A covered wagon was waiting to carry him to the castle. He felt the jolts as it bumped along a cobbled way. Then there came a terrible sound: the dull boom the great gates made as they swung shut behind him.

The wagon halted, and he was manhandled out and up a narrow spiral staircase. Bruised and battered from the knocks he took on the way, he was finally flung down onto the floor of a room at the very top of what he thought must be the castle's highest tower. There his bonds were cut and the gag pulled from his mouth. Then his captors left him, clanging shut a heavy, iron-studded oak door behind them.

Robin looked around him. He was in a circular chamber about six paces across, with straw scattered on the bare stone floor but no furnishing of any kind. There were three narrow windows, but a quick look was enough to show they opened up onto a sheer drop of more than a hundred feet.

Things looked bad, but Robin still had one hope left. In the confusion of the arrest, the soldiers had forgotten to remove the small hunting horn he always carried on his belt, hidden under the cloak he was wearing. Now he raised it to his lips. He managed to blow three blasts before the door of the prison swung open and the guards rushed in to overpower him.

As they held him down, another figure followed them into the room. It was the Sheriff. He watched as the soldiers tore the horn from Robin's grasp and flung it across the chamber. Then he stepped over to stare down on the captive as they fought with him.

"Robert of Locksley, as I live and breathe!" he said in a low voice. "But I never for a moment doubted it."

"You'll never keep me here," Robin said defiantly. "My men will come and get me."

"They'll never have the

chance." The Sheriff's voice was flat, almost matter-of-fact. "You'll be dead tomorrow. But we're not going to kill you fast. You've caused us too much trouble for that."

He stopped speaking and a new expression spread across his face. Robin realized he was grinning, but in a horribly mirthless manner. "We're going to give you an archer's death," the Sheriff continued. "First we'll cut off your fingers, to stop you from drawing a bow. Then we'll blind you with red-hot irons, so you can no longer see a target. And maybe then we'll give you the Silver Arrow ~ in the heart at fifty paces."

"You'll pay for every scratch you leave on me," Robin hissed. But the Sheriff wasn't listening. He had left the chamber, waving the soldiers out after him. Robin grabbed his hunting horn from the floor and rushed to follow, but the great oak door clanged firmly shut in his face.

Alone in the tower that evening, Robin looked out over the darkening town, feeling despair creep up on him. He had hoped to hear an answering horn-blast to show that Little John or Will Scarlett had at least heard his call, but none had come.

He stood at the window until the sun went down, knowing that he might never see it set again. Then, as the shadows lengthened across the room, he lay down on the straw and gazed up at the stone ceiling above him. Usually projects and plans filled his racing brain, but now he could think of nothing except for the horrors awaiting him the next morning.

Danger Time

Robin tossed and turned on the straw for what seemed like hours before finally dropping off into a fitful sleep. Even then, bad dreams tormented him. He kept seeing  himself in the castle dungeons, strapped to some terrible machine, with the Sheriff's thin-lipped face gazing down at 'him. The night brought him little rest.

He woke with a start to find the light of dawn filtering through the windows. He was sure he'd heard something, but at first he couldn't work out what it was. Then it came again. It was the sound of a hunting horn, clear and shrill. He leaped to his feet, suddenly full of hope. Maybe Will and Little John hadn't given up on him after all!

A third blast sounded. He rushed to a window to try to spot his friends ~ then jumped back as an arrow came whistling in and thudded against the ceiling.

Picking himself up, Robin saw that a length of rope was fastened to the shaft with twine. The rope was strong enough to take a man's weight ~ and it snaked outside toward freedom.

Cautiously, Robin risked another peek out of the window. The arrow had been fired from the far side of the tower ~ the side that lay beyond the castle walls. The rope fell away down the side of the building toward two figures in Lincoln green who were waving at him urgently. They looked as small as toys from that height, but Robin could recognize the taller of the two as Little John.

Robin looked around the room for something to tie the rope to. There was an iron ring on the door that looked solid enough. He threaded the end through and knotted it several times. Then, after tugging with all his might to check that the knot was secure, he took a firm grip and stepped up onto the window ledge.

Robin was a brave man, but he had one weakness. Sheer drops had always terrified him. Now the height almost took his breath away. For a split second he froze, but then the thought of the Sheriff's torturers spurred him on. Closing his eyes, he stepped off the ledge into emptiness.

The rope he clung to was his lifeline, and he tried to clear his mind of everything except climbing down it. Slowly he descended, hand over hand over hand over hand, until his palms were raw from the rubbing of the rope and his knees and ankles ached from gripping it.

Robin was concentrating so hard that the thought of what would happen when the castle guards realized he was getting away hardly crossed his mind. He was already halfway down before it dawned on him that no one had given the alarm. He'd barely had time to bless his luck when a shout went up from a sentry posted on the castle wall. The guards on the gate took up the cry, and in seconds he could hear a hubbub as guards and soldiers poured out into the castle yard to find out what was happening.

He was in no immediate danger, for the tower cut him off from the soldiers; its projecting corners even put him out of arrow-range of the sentries on the walls. But then the rope jolted abruptly, and he realized the guards in the tower must have burst into the room in which he had been held. His heart sank. All they had to do was cut the rope, and he was a dead man.

But, amazingly, the rope remained uncut. Instead, the guards contented themselves with shooting arrows at him. Firing as they were from the cramped window ledge, where there wasn't enough room to aim or draw a bow properly, the soldiers never came close to their mark. To make their task harder, Little John and his companion let off a stream of arrows of their own at the window.

At the time, Robin couldn't even imagine why his life had been spared. It was only afterward that it dawned on him that orders must have been given for him to be taken alive. Although the guards would have been happy enough to have wounded him, they didn't want to see him plunge to his doom in the castle yard. A quick death like that would never have satisfied the Sheriff, who had

THE ROPE HE CLUNG TO WAS HIS LIFELINE

set his heart on a more drawn-out revenge.

Robin's knees scraped against stone. Looking down, he saw that Little John had pulled the rope up close against the wall to protect him better. He slid down to the end and dropped to the ground. Above him, he could hear the sentries shouting a warning that he was getting away.

The three outlaws ran along the base of the tower, keeping out of sight of the soldiers. There were horses tethered and waiting at the angle of the wall. Once he was in the saddle, Robin turned to thank Will Scarlett, only to find it wasn't Will at all. It was Marian. Robin's jaw dropped. She grinned at him.

"You should have known I'd come," she said. "Did you think I'd leave you for the Sheriff?" There was no time for explanations, so Robin simply shook his head in amazement. The three urged their horses on over the open ground that lay between the castle walls and the fields beyond. They were soon out of range of the handful of arrows the soldiers loosed after them.

But Robin knew their problems weren't over yet, and he was soon proved right. They had barely reached the road that led to Sherwood when, cresting a small hill, they found themselves gazing down on a company of soldiers riding along it toward them.

The men had evidently been dispatched by the Sheriff to patrol the route between the castle and the forest.

A cry from the ranks warned the outlaws that they had been spotted. There wasn't a moment to lose. The three wheeled their horses back toward the fields. Glancing over his shoulder toward the town, Robin saw horsemen there too, streaming out of the city gates. The hunt was on, and he and his friends were the quarry.

The outlaws set off at a gallop across the grass. If they could only keep far enough ahead of the soldiers across three or four fields, they would be able to swing across the path of their pursuers and reach the safety of the forest. Given luck, they'd be home and dry, leaving the Sheriff's men to regret the day they thought they could outride the Sherwood horsemen.

But just as everything seemed to be going well, disaster struck. Little John's horse stumbled over a rabbit hole. It managed to keep on going, but it was obviously injured. It would never outpace the Sheriff's men to the wood. Robin thought fast. There was a river

nearby, and for the time being they were out of sight of the soldiers, hidden by a rise in the ground. Coming to a quick decision, Robin pulled his horse away from Sherwood and rode toward the riverbank, shouting to the others to follow him.

They reached the stream without being spotted. Once they had arrived there, high banks and undergrowth provided extra cover. The three rode upstream in the water for a couple of hundred yards to a place where a small thicket grew on the far bank. Then Robin told Little John to dismount.

The big man did as he was told without asking questions. Knee deep in water, he made no complaint when Robin shooed the lamed horse away into the trees. But he shook his head despairingly when Robin told him to climb up onto his mount.

"Let me hide here," he said. "No horse would get far carrying the two of us."

"We're not going far," Robin told him tersely. "When the Sheriff's men see the hoofprints, they'll think we've split up. It's our best chance to get them off our trail."

With just two horses between them now, the three continued up the stream. What Robin had remembered was that the minstrel Alan-a-Dale, a longtime friend of the outlaws, lived with his wife only half a mile away in a cottage near the river. If he and his companions could reach the house without being spotted, they could lie low there overnight and make their way to Sherwood in relative safety before dawn the next morning.

They rode along in silence, fearing that the least noise might alert the soldiers. The only sound was the soft splash the horses' hooves made as they broke the water's surface.

A couple of hundred yards short of their destination, the three reached a spot where the banks rose up above their heads on either side of the river. The current had cut away the earth beneath, forming an overhang whose underside was almost completely hidden. They tethered the horses there, out of sight, then continued on foot toward the cottage.

Alan-a-Dale and his wife couldn't have been more surprised to see Robin. They had only just heard that he had been captured, and had been grieving for him. They didn't need to be asked to give help, even though they were risking their lives by offering it.

The minstrel led the three to a barn in the yard at the back of the cottage. He pointed at the straw piled thickly on the floor.

"Hide in there," he said. "It won't be very comfortable, but it's the best I can manage."

The three outlaws burrowed deep into the hay. Alan-a-Dale waited to check that they were completely covered, then left, promising to come back once he was sure the coast was clear.

❦❦❦❦❦❦❦❦❦❦❦

And so the waiting began. It was hot and damp under the hay, and the close, stuffy air made breathing difficult. Throughout the long day they lay sweltering, scratched and chafed by the dry straw yet hardly daring to move in case the Sheriff's men were nearby.

Sometime in the afternoon they heard the sound of horses' hooves approaching the cottage. For a few terrible minutes they hardly dared draw their breath, thinking that they must be discovered. Then the riders clattered away down the lane again. They realized they'd had a lucky escape; the soldiers must have been content just to look inside the cottage.

Darkness had fallen before Alan came out again. He still kept his voice to a whisper. But he knew they hadn't had anything to eat all day, and he suggested they might like to come to the cottage for a meal. They hardly needed encouraging. They were all so hungry they'd have gone even if they had known that the Sheriff of Nottingham in person was combing the neighborhood for them.

It was a sober dinner, for even though the door was bolted and the windows shuttered, Robin insisted that the guests stay silent. They ate well, then remained quietly in the cottage, always on the alert for the sound of the soldiers returning.

As the evening wore on into night, the three finally began to relax a little. It seemed unlikely the Sheriff would keep his men out so late, even with Robin Hood on the run. It looked as though the worst might be over. Time passed without any further alarms.

❦❦❦❦❦❦❦❦❦❦❦

Shortly before midnight, Robin asked Little John to go to the stream and fetch the horses. He planned to set out at first light, aiming to reach Sherwood before the hunters were out looking for them. Robin's main worry during the long hours of waiting had been that their mounts might have been discovered, so he was relieved when the big man came back ten minutes later leading both horses by the bridle. Meanwhile Alan had offered to lend the outlaws his own mare for the journey. He told them he would come to Sherwood to collect her once all the commotion had died down.

Alan and the outlaws were enjoying the luxury of a quiet conversation when Robin suddenly held up his hand for silence. He was sure he'd heard a sound outside: some movement, something stirring. He tiptoed over to the window and abruptly threw open the shutters.

The light of the rushes Alan was burning for his guests streamed out into the darkness. For a split second it fell on something white. Whatever it was, it had no sooner been glimpsed than it vanished back into the blackness. Had it been a face? Instinctively, Robin drew his sword, but no sound broke the stillness beyond the walls of the cottage. Troubled, Robin looked over to Marian. He saw she was shaking.

"What was it?" he asked.

"Guy," she said dully, but with absolute certainty in her voice. "Guy of Gisborne. He must have been watching the horses."

The words were still sinking in when something struck the outer door of the house so hard that the walls shuddered.

"To your weapons!" Robin shouted. "It's Guy's men. They're trying to break down the door." Little John and Marian seized their bows, and Alan thrust another into Robin's hand. Searching desperately, the minstrel managed to turn up a pair of rusty swords and a handful of kitchen knives. It wasn't much of an armory with which to take on mailed knights.

Robin sent Alan and his wife to the back of the house, where they would be in less immediate danger. Then the outlaws pushed what furniture there was in the room up against the door to barricade it against the battering the soldiers were giving it. As they were doing so, the shutters of the main window burst open. A hail of arrows flew in, rattling against the ceiling.

The three flattened themselves against the walls, trying to keep out of reach of the missiles. Outside they could hear the sound of many armed men. Guy of Gisborne's voice rose above the clamor, shouting orders. Robin worked his way around to the open window, ducking out of cover to fire arrows of his own whenever he could see a target. He reckoned there were at least twenty men attacking the house.

Things already looked bad when a smell of burning warned him they were about to get a great deal worse. He realized to his horror that Guy's men must have set the roof-thatch on fire with flaming arrows. That settled it: they would have to abandon the cottage or see it become their funeral pyre. Their only hope was to reach the horses in the yard and make a dash for the river.

Robin shouted to the others to fall back into the yard. He planned to stay in the cottage and hold the attackers at bay for as long as possible while his companions made their getaway. But they had only three horses between them. Marian would have to take one, he decided, and Alan-a-Dale and his wife would need the second. He and Little John would have to take their chances on the remaining mount, trusting to the darkness beyond the flames' glow as their best hope of safety.

To pin the attackers down while Marian got Alan and his wife away, Robin loosed a stream of arrows out into the darkness. The answering fire was just as fierce. As he turned to reach for a fresh quiver, Robin felt a blow that sent him reeling. Steadying himself against a wall, he put a hand to his head and felt something warm and sticky. It was blood. An arrow had gashed his forehead. It was only a flesh wound, but it seemed long and deep. But he couldn't worry about that now. He could hear Little John screaming from the yard that the others had gone and they wouldn't have another chance to follow them.

Robin staggered out of the house with blood streaming down his face. But as he reached the yard, disaster struck again. The thatch of the roof, which had so far been smoldering quietly, suddenly flared up into a wall of flame. The waiting horse panicked, rearing up on its hind legs. Then, despite Little John's frantic attempts to control it, it took off at a gallop, leaping the gate out of the yard and disappearing with its rider into the blackness. Robin gazed after it wildly. He knew his last chance of escape had gone with it.

Despairingly, he looked around him. The yard was lit up by the burning building as brightly as by the light of day. The soldiers had seen him by now, and they were moving toward him. He felt weak and

tired and helpless, drained by too much bad luck. Summoning all his courage for a last time, he drew his sword and turned to face the enemy. At least he meant to go down fighting.

The soldiers were spreading out to encircle him. He could see the light of the flames glinting off their armor as they moved to cut him off from the river. Guy of Gisborne was in the center, motioning with his sword. At his bidding, the ring of steel around Robin began to tighten.

Then, when Robin's last hope seemed to have gone, something quite extraordinary happened. Robin heard a noise behind him, coming from the direction of the burning cottage. He turned, expecting to see more soldiers. Instead, he gazed open-mouthed as a gigantic figure loomed into view, coming, it seemed, from the very heart of the smoke and flames. It was a knight clad from head to foot in black armor, and he was swooping down on Robin on an enormous ebony charger. His sword was unsheathed and he was brandishing it above his head, pointed forward in the attack position.

The apparition was so strange that Robin, dazed by his wound,

wondered for a split second if maybe it was Death itself finally coming to claim him. But he had little time to worry, for in an instant the horseman was upon him. Only instead of striking him down with the flashing blade, the Black Knight leaned forward toward him. With one sweep of his mighty arm, he snatched Robin up and lifted him into the saddle.

With Robin clutching desperately to its mane, the great horse rushed on toward the river, scattering Guy's men before it as it went. Robin heard their angry cries as the charger plunged on into the darkness. Faint now from loss of blood, he could also dimly make out the pattering sound the soldiers' arrows made as they bounced harmlessly off the broad, armored back of his mysterious deliverer.

Then they were away and free. The last thing he was aware of was his rescuer heaving him more securely onto the neck of the horse and holding him there with a firm, protective hand. He slumped forward against the charger's neck. For a time he listened to the horse's panting as it rushed onward through the night. Then everything went black and he lost consciousness.

A GIGANTIC FIGURE LOOMED INTO VIEW

THE FINAL CHALLENGE PART 3:
THE RETURN OF THE BLACK KNIGHT

When Robin came to, the sun was high in the sky and he was alone. He was lying in a thicket, hidden by the undergrowth in a ring of bushes; the Black Knight ~ if it was the Black Knight who had put him there ~ had taken care that he should not be found. He raised his hand to his throbbing head, and found that his wound had been bound up with a strip of cloth. He thought he had his rescuer to thank for that as well.

Stepping out of the bushes, he soon realized where he was. The thicket was inside Sherwood Forest, only about a mile from the camp. He looked around for any sign of his rescuer, but could see none. Baffled by what had happened, he limped off to rejoin his men.

He arrived to find the camp mourning his loss. Alan-a-Dale, his wife and Marian had all managed to get back safely. So had Little John, with the story of how Robin had been left at the blazing cottage. The outlaws were the more delighted to see him because they had given him up for dead. The story of his escape seemed like a miracle.

But there wasn't much time for talking about the past. Robin could imagine only too well the Sheriff's fury when he heard his greatest enemy had slipped through his grasp. He thought there would be a raid on the camp, probably that very morning.

Robin sent out scouts to the forest edge, then called the rest of the men together. There were about sixty outlaws in all, and he climbed up onto a rocky outcrop to address them.

"By rights I shouldn't be here this morning," he told them. "Death was expecting me yesterday, and it's only thanks to Marian and Little John that I disappointed him. I'm still alive in spite of everything, though, and I mean to stay that way. But the Sheriff may have other ideas. He won't take my escape lying down. We have to prepare for an attack. You all know what you have to do. Do it fast, and do it well."

Within seconds the area around the clearing was a hive of activity. Some of the men were digging furiously. Others were rushing back and forth carrying bundles of twigs almost as big as they were, or else unreeling massive balls of twine. Archers took up stations in the treetops, choosing spots among the branches that gave them a clear view of the forest floor below.

The outlaws were well drilled, for they had often practiced for such an emergency. In less than an hour they were ready, which was just as well, for the last snares were hardly in place when the sound of galloping hooves reached the glade. It was one of the scouts returning to give warning that a small army of mounted men was moving into the forest.

Robin shouted an order and the men headed for their posts. Some climbed up trees lining the main track into the clearing.

Others hid themselves in the undergrowth by the roadside.

The men crouched in their hiding places, still and tense. For what seemed like an eternity, they could hear nothing but the singing of the birds in the trees around the clearing. Then came another sound. It was a faint jingling, coming toward them from along the forest track. No one needed to be told it was the noise of armored men on horseback.

In another minute, the archers in the treetops could see the head of the column. The soldiers were riding three abreast. Sunlight filtering through the leaves glinted on chainmail. At the horsemen's sides swung swords and daggers.

From a lookout in the trees Robin surveyed the approaching column. It was by far the biggest force the Sheriff had ever ordered into Sherwood. He decided more than a hundred men had been sent against them. Midway along its length rode a figure clad from head to foot in armor. Robin had no trouble in recognizing the knight as Guy of Gisborne.

By now the first soldiers had almost reached the clearing. But before they got there, the column was brought to an unceremonious halt. The outlaws had booby-trapped the paths with trenches, disguised by coverings of earth. The first horses stumbled into one of the traps, and a couple of the riders were thrown. The other soldiers reined in their mounts, unsure what was happening.

It was the sign the outlaws had been waiting for. Suddenly the forest exploded into action. Men hidden in the branches above the track cast nets down on the horses stalled beneath them. Grappling-hooks emerged from the under-growth to pull soldiers down from their mounts. And from the tops of all the surrounding trees a hail of arrows rained down upon the column.

The Sheriff's men were taken by surprise. The horsemen at the rear of the line set off through the trees to help their comrades under attack at its head. But the out-laws had done their work well. Tripwires stretched between the trunks and holes dug in the ground soon sent them tumbling. Within minutes the forest was full of horses that had lost their riders, and the column that had ridden so proudly into Sherwood was in total disarray.

Seeing the shambles around him, Guy barked out an order to retreat. Those soldiers who were still mounted reined their horses in and turned back along the path by which they

had come. The rest struggled after them on foot, many with blood streaming from wounds. The outlaws were left in control of the clearing.

A cheer went up around the glade at the sight of the departing soldiers. Outlaws clambered down the trees and emerged from the bushes to hug one another and wave their weapons in the air in delight. They quieted down quickly enough, though, when Robin stepped forward and gestured for silence.

"Well done," he told them. "We've shown Guy and his men what we're made of, and they won't forget it. But don't start celebrating too soon. The battle isn't over yet. They've only withdrawn to regroup. They'll be back before the day's out to finish what they've started. And this time it won't be so easy to catch them unaware."

Sobered by Robin's speech, the men started preparing for another fight to come. They sharpened their swords and refilled their quivers with arrows. Those who had an appetite found the time to swallow down some food, knowing they might not have the chance later. The outlaws laughed to see Friar Tuck, with armor strapped over his monk's robes, devouring half a ham. Fighting only seemed to make him hungrier.

Time passed, and the outlaws waited. Robin had sent out

scouts again with instructions to return as soon as they saw the soldiers on the move, but none came back. It was a hot day, and as the sun reached its peak and then gradually started to go down behind the treetops, some of the outlaws began to hope that maybe Guy's men had had enough. Perhaps they wouldn't be coming back after all.

But then the first of the scouts rode up to report that he had seen the soldiers regrouping on the forest's edge. From that time on, a steady stream of riders returned with news of their movements: they had swung around to the north; they were advancing on the camp; they were only minutes away.

The men had taken up new positions to meet the new threat. Robin himself was perched in the branches of a tree that gave him a good view of the direction from which Guy's men were coming. He waited for the familiar jingling of oncoming horsemen. But it never came. Instead, the sound he eventually heard was more of a crackling and rustling. Then he saw the first of the troops, and the sight confirmed what he had feared: they had dismounted and were

approaching the camp on foot. That would make them harder to beat in the forest.

As the soldiers came nearer, they spread out into a long line. Armed men checked every thicket and piece of undergrowth for ambushers. Guy was taking no chances. His men were combing the forest like beaters raising game for a hunt.

Robin knew at once that surprise tactics wouldn't work against this new assault. He shouted a warning, and the men concealed in the path of the advancing troops rose up from their hiding places. Against foot soldiers their orders were to keep moving. Meanwhile the archers in the treetops kept up a steady fire.

For well over an hour the two sides played cat and mouse with one another. Guy's men moved forward in line, driving the outlaws from their path. But Robin and his men would disappear off among the trees only to slip around and fire at the soldiers from behind. Try as they might, Guy's men could not get their opponents to fight hand to hand in the kind of battle that, with more men and better armor, they knew they could win.

Of all Robin's fighters, none was faster or more nimble on the attack than the youngest, Dickon. Instead of a bow, he used a slingshot as his weapon. His aim was deadly; he could stun a man from fifty paces. And each time a stone struck home, he'd shout defiantly, "That one's for my father!"

Hit-and-run fighting was a dangerous game, and there were soon people wounded on both sides. Robin's bowmen managed to pick off some of the soldiers despite the armor protecting them. But the outlaws suffered too. Robin winced when he saw William of Goldsborough, the man who had helped him rescue Will Scarlett, go down with an arrow in the arm.

Will himself was always in the thick of the fighting, wielding a heavy, double-edged sword. He was so blind to danger that at one time he found himself trapped, pinned by two of Guy's men against a tree. He managed to bring one of them down, but as he struggled with that soldier on the ground, the other reared above him, ready to deliver a fatal blow. Just in time, an arrow caught the soldier's arm, knocking him off

balance and giving Will the chance to get away.

He looked around for the archer who had saved him, and saw a solitary bowman crouched high in a tree. He raised a hand in salute, shouting:

"You're quite a marksman."

"Markswoman, you mean," the archer called back. Doffing her cap, she shook out long brown hair. It was Marian.

By then it was late afternoon and the sun had long since gone down behind the treetops. Robin was beginning to think the fighting might simply peter out with the fall of darkness when he noticed a cluster of Guy's men kneeling on the ground. There was a spark, then smoke began to curl lazily into the evening air. Fire! Having failed to fight the outlaws to a standstill, the soldiers evidently meant to burn them out.

Men with flaming branches ran between the trees, setting the undergrowth on fire. Soon the blaze was spreading rapidly toward the clearing. Meanwhile a line of armed men started to move around to cut off escape from the other side. Robin's men were in danger of getting trapped between a wall of fire and a ring of steel.

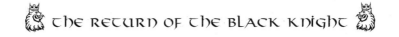

Things looked bad for the outlaws. Bowmen were scrambling down from the treetops to avoid getting caught in the blaze. The men were falling back in confusion. It only needed one or two to panic, and the retreat could easily turn into a disorderly stampede. Robin saw the danger, and rushed forward to rally the outlaws.

And then, as the battle hung in the balance, the men heard the sound of a hunting-horn calling from the depth of the forest behind them. They turned around in surprise to see the Black Knight, in full armor, moving up the track toward them.

The effect was electric. Everyone in Robin's ranks had heard what had happened the night before. They fell away to the side of the track, clearing a way for the charging knight. He thundered past them and on toward the center of the enemy line. The line wavered, then broke. It seemed that Guy's men too had heard about the Black Knight, and the sudden sight of him spread terror among them. The men facing him turned and ran.

Smashing through the ranks, the knight careened onward and disappeared among the trees. Seeing the danger to his line, Guy of Gisborne spurred his mount into the gap and managed to hold his force together. But the damage had been done. His soldiers were on the defensive now, and Robin only needed to press home his advantage. Meanwhile, untended by the fire starters who had dropped their branches to run for their weapons, the fire reached the clearing and then sputtered out.

Robin now had a plan in mind to finish off Guy's forces.

He knew that there was a stream not far away where river mist tended to rise in the evenings. Now he saw that the soldiers were falling back toward it. He ran forward to wave his men on, urging them to make one final effort to push the foe back into the haze.

At this crucial moment, two huge figures strode forward to answer his call. Little John and Friar Tuck took up position side by side. Though neither was aware of what Robin had in mind, they knew he needed them and that was enough. Shoulder to shoulder with him, the two big men led the advance, and the other outlaws, seeing Guy's men giving way before them, soon joined in behind.

Step by step Guy's forces moved back toward the water. They were so busy defending themselves from the onslaught that they never even noticed the screen of fog behind them ~ or the spongy quagmire of marshy ground that lay hidden beneath it.

The retreating soldiers were already ankle-deep in slime before they realized the danger. Robin's men were pressing hard upon them, so in desperation they turned toward the stream to find a way out of the mud that was holding them back. But the further they went, the deeper the ooze became. Soon the sludge was up to their knees and it was becoming difficult for them to move. Meanwhile, Robin's bow-men, safely planted on dry ground, sent volley after volley of arrows into their ranks.

When they finally reached the stream itself, the Sheriff's men

GUY TOOK A LAST, WILD SWING

were able to regain their footing on the firm, pebbly bed. But by then they had had enough. They dropped their weapons and ran off through the water, trusting to the mist to cover their escape. Robin was happy enough to let them go. This time he didn't think they'd be back.

But there was one man he didn't want to get away. Guy of Gisborne's horse had become trapped in the mud and had fallen, throwing its rider. Now Guy emerged from the mist on foot. He had lost the plumed crest from his helmet, and his armor was smeared with dripping slime. But his sword was drawn, and there was the courage of desperation in his eyes.

Gesturing to the other men to stand back, Robin moved toward him. The two men stood face to face.

"We have scores to settle," he told his old enemy, speaking quietly but with steely determination in his voice. "You stole my house, and you tried to steal my wife. Now it's time to pay your debts." Then he drew his sword. It had come to single combat at last.

Guy was in full chainmail while Robin only wore a leather chest guard. His head and limbs were uncovered, but the lighter body-covering made him the more agile, and he seemed to the onlookers almost to dance out of reach of his tired foe, whose desperate, two-handed lunges kept going wide of the mark.

In contrast, Robin landed many blows on his enemy's armor without doing more than scratching the steel. But then Guy took a last, wild swing and stumbled, and Robin, fast as a hawk, plunged his blade through the join where helmet and armor met. With a terrible cry the knight fell, and he did not rise again. Guy of Gisborne was dead.

A roar went up from the outlaws, and they rushed forward to lift Robin onto their shoulders. But he raised a hand to stop them. For a little way off, at the very edge of the band of mist rising from the river, the Black Knight sat silently on his charger. Now Robin went to pay his respects to the man who had saved his life.

He walked over and raised a hand in greeting. But then the knight raised his visor. Robin stared into his face, then fell to his knees, bowing his head. Silently, the other outlaws followed him.

THEY WERE KNEELING TO THEIR RIGHTFUL KING

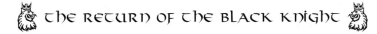

They were kneeling to their rightful king, Richard Lionheart, back from the Crusades at last.

Humbly, Robin started to ask the king's pardon for the wrongs his men had done while he was away: the deer they had poached in his forests and the purses they had taken from travelers on his highway. But Richard quickly stopped him.

"I heard many things of Robin Hood while I was on my travels," he said. "News of your adventures reached us even in the Holy Land. There were those who claimed you were a common thief and vagabond who only deserved hanging from the kingdom's highest tree. But others told me I had no more loyal follower in England. And that is why I came to Sherwood ~ to find out the truth. It didn't take me long to learn which side I should believe. And that was just as well, because there wasn't any time to lose. Otherwise I might have been too late to come to the aid of an honest man and a friend."

The outlaws roared their approval, and when the king went on to say that all Robin's lands and titles would be restored to him, the whole clearing rang with their cheers. Then he added that any of his men who now wished to enter the Lionheart's service would be well rewarded for doing so, and their happiness was complete. The forest echoed to the ovation they gave him.

When the king had finished speaking, Friar Tuck stepped forward respectfully to remind Robert of Locksley, as he was once again, of some important, unfinished business. Had he not promised that the marriage ceremony so rudely interrupted all those months ago would be completed as soon as the Lionheart was back in his own lands?

Robin turned to look for Marian and found her already at his side. There was no father to give the bride away, but at Robin's request Little John stepped forward, looking solemn and self-conscious, to act as best man. And there, under the greenwood trees, they were married by Friar Tuck. The king himself was the first to bless the match.

It was time for celebration, but there was still important business to be done first. The King had scores to settle with the Sheriff of Nottingham, and he needed Robin's men to help him. It was a task the

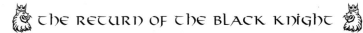

fighters ~ outlaws no more ~ were only too happy to accomplish.

And so the men prepared to take their leave of Sherwood. The forest had been their home for so long that there was more than a little sadness in the thought of leaving its clearings and thickets, even for the comforts of a warm home and a soft bed. But they also knew that, for the meanwhile at least, the time for sleeping out under the stars lay behind them.

So as twilight deepened over the countryside, they took the road for Nottingham and rode out of the forest for the last time. The King was at their head, and Robin at his side. Ahead of them a new life was opening. First they had to free a city; and after that a whole kingdom waited to be reclaimed.

THE END

WHO WAS ROBIN HOOD?

EARLIEST MENTION

No one knows for sure if there ever was a real Robin Hood. The earliest surviving mention of him is in one of the great English poems of the Middle Ages, *Piers Plowman* by William Langland. In the poem, a character who represents Sloth (laziness) says he doesn't know how to say his prayers very well, but he does know the rhymes of Robin Hood. This suggests that by 1377, when the poem was written, stories about Robin were already popular, and also that they were considered by some people as simply a way of wasting time – rather like watching too much television today.

THE BALLADS

The sort of "rhymes" that Langland no doubt had in mind were ballads - stories sung by minstrels at inns and markets and in noblemen's halls. Five early Robin Hood ballads have survived, and between them they provide us with most of what we know of the original Robin. Sometimes ballads concerned real people and sometimes they were about characters that the minstrels had made up. This explains why it is so difficult to know whether there ever was a real-life Robin Hood.

ROBIN THE ROBBER

The Robin Hood of the early ballads is in some ways very like the character we know today. At least one of the stories in this book, *Paying Back Debts*, draws closely on a plot from a ballad called *A Lytell Gest of Robyn Hode*, which was first put into print in 1492. In other respects though, the original Robin is very different. He is neither a peasant, nor (as in this book) a lord robbed of his rights. Instead he is a yeoman (a small landholder), who is forced to become an outlaw for reasons that none of the surviving ballads explains. He robs from the rich, and particularly from monasteries and bishops – the Church was famously wealthy at this time. He also poaches the king's deer. But there is no mention of him helping the poor.

A SHERWOOD SETTING?

The big surprise of the early ballads is their setting. Although Sherwood Forest features in several of them, and the Sheriff of Nottingham is the main villain, so too does the district of Barnsdale, between Doncaster and Wakefield in South Yorkshire. In one of the ballads, Robin specifically calls himself "Robin of Barnsdale."

THE BARNSDALE OUTLAWS

Barnsdale was an area around the Great North Road (now the A1 from London), and the outlaws in the ballads stopped travelers who were journeying along it. In one story, Robin tells Little John to "walk up to Sayles", which historians think was the area known today as Sayles Plantation, near Wentbridge. Visitors to the area can still see, in a field near the crossroads at Barnsdale Bar, a stone monument, set up in the 18th century to mark a site known locally as Robin Hood's Well. Barnsdale lies only 48 kilometers (30 miles), or a day's ride, from the northern tip of Sherwood Forest, so it is possible that one band of outlaws could have operated in both areas.

Certainly both districts were known as dangerous territory at the time. There are records of prisoners' guards being doubled for safety's sake as they passed through Barnsdale. As for Sherwood, a charter of Prince John's day grants the officer in charge of the forest all the possessions of robbers and poachers caught within its bounds.

hood and hunter

The first serious attempt to find a real Robin Hood in the historical records was made by a scholar called Joseph Hunter in 1852. He decided that the one event in the ballads that could definitely be tracked down in the available documents was a reference to "Edward our comely king" traveling through the northern forests and ending up in Nottingham, where he encounters Robin Hood. The only royal tour which Hunter could find to fit the bill was made by Edward II in 1323. Checking the records, Hunter then found mention of a 'Robyn Hode' who worked for the king as a porter in the following year, 1324. Hunter suggested that this man might have been the outlaw, who made peace with the king on the royal tour and was rewarded with a position in his household.

pub proof

Other historians have challenged Hunter's theory. They think that the real Robin, if there was one, must have lived earlier than Edward II's reign. Records show that there was already a pub in London called the Robin Hood in 1294 (13 years before Edward II came to the throne). Scholars searching the records have also found people giving "Robinhood" as their surname or nickname from about the same time.

the chronicles

There is also the evidence of the chronicles - early histories made up of lists of events and the years in which they were thought to have happened. Of the three chronicles that mention Robin Hood, one puts him in the 1280s and another in the 1260s. The third – written by a man called John Major – is the first source to date the outlaw to Richard the Lionheart's reign. According to Major, Robin and his band were at work in the years 1193 and 1194, when Richard was in the Holy Land. Each of the chronicles was written well over a hundred years after the dates given for Robin, so all may have been based on inaccurate information.

atmospheric argument

Probably the best argument put forward by people who think that Robin really existed is the nature of the ballads themselves. The atmosphere of the stories is unusually realistic. Even though he is an exceptionally gifted archer, Robin is not portrayed as a Superman, with more-than-human powers, and he isn't made to fight monsters or giants, as other legendary medieval heroes were. In the Barnsdale stories in particular, he seems to be linked to a real district, whose place-names are still on the map. We also know that there were actual families called Hood in the area at the time.

the harsh truth

In the long run, it probably doesn't much matter whether Robin Hood really existed or not. Even if there was an actual Robin Hood, the chances are that he had very little in common with the hero of the stories. There was not much that was exciting or romantic about the life of a genuine fugitive in the Middle Ages, and much that was savage, harsh and cruel. If the real Robin could be transported by some magical time-machine into the present day, it is unlikely that many of his admirers would recognize him.

rebel appeal

More important to the legend is what generations of singers, writers, performers and artists have done with Robin. Over the centuries, they thought up new plots and added extra characters to the stories, making them less true to the original as they did so, but also keeping them alive for fresh generations to enjoy.

As early as the 15th century, actors dressed up as Robin Hood and his companions were a regular part of the May Day festivities that celebrated the coming of spring each year. In 1515, courtiers of Henry VIII staged a pageant in which members of the royal guard, in the costume of the outlaws, invited the king and his queen to dine on venison in a forest shelter made of branches and decorated with flowers and sweet-smelling herbs. A hundred years later, storytellers were thinking up new adventures for the band, some of which in time themselves became part of the legend. In the present century, Robin was born again as a hero of pantomimes and films. What hasn't changed is the idea of a group of comrades living together in the forest and doing battle against a hostile and unjust outside world. The story of Robin Hood and his band appeals to the rebel in all of us, and no doubt still will in another 500 years.

BOOKS TO READ

The Adventures of Robin Hood by Roger Lancelyn Green (Puffin 1984) – A standard retelling of the stories, sticking closely to the original tales.

Robin of Sherwood by Richard Carpenter (Puffin, 1990) – A reworking of the legend by the man who devised the *Robin of Sherwood* TV series.

Robin Hood by J.C. Holt (Thames & Hudson, 1982) – The best factual introduction, written by a medieval historian.

The True History of Robin Hood by J.W. Walker (1952) – An attempt to identify the real Robin by searching local records.

Rymes of Robin Hood: An Introduction to the English Outlaw by R.B. Dobson and J. Taylor (1976) – A historical survey, with a selection of the early ballads.

THE CAST OF CHARACTERS

One of the special things about the Robin Hood saga is that it has always featured not just a single hero but a whole cast of characters, some good and some bad. Here's how some of the other characters first made their appearance.

LITTLE JOHN

One of the original characters. He is in fact the real hero of *Robin Hood and the Monk*, the earliest of all the ballads. In it he rescues Robin from the clutches of the Sheriff of Nottingham, by killing and then taking the place of the messenger sent to carry news of the outlaw's capture to the king. Later Robin seeks to repay him by offering him command of the outlaw band, only to have the suggestion turned down. But the story of his fight against Robin at the bridge doesn't appear until the 18th century.

WILL SCARLETT

One of the original characters, though known at first as Will Scarlok or Will Scathelocke. In one of the ballads he warns Robin not to go to Kirklees Priory in Yorkshire, where the outlaw eventually meets his death; in another he has to flee for his life from the Sheriff's men.

THE MILLER'S SON (DICKON)

One of the original characters. In *Robin Hood and the Monk*, he is Little John's helper, killing the messenger's page to carry through the impersonation that saves Robin.

FRIAR TUCK

First mentioned in a fragment of a play about Robin Hood dating from around 1475. But before that time, a real outlaw calling himself Friar Tuck is known to have operated in the counties of Surrey and Sussex. He and his followers hunted without permission, burned foresters' lodges, and were charged with robbery and killing. Historians argue over whether this man, whose real name was Robert Stafford and who had been chaplain of Lindfield in Sussex, borrowed the name from the Robin Hood stories, or whether the Friar Tuck of the stories was based on him. As things stand, it seems more likely that there was a 'real' Friar Tuck than a 'real' Robin Hood.